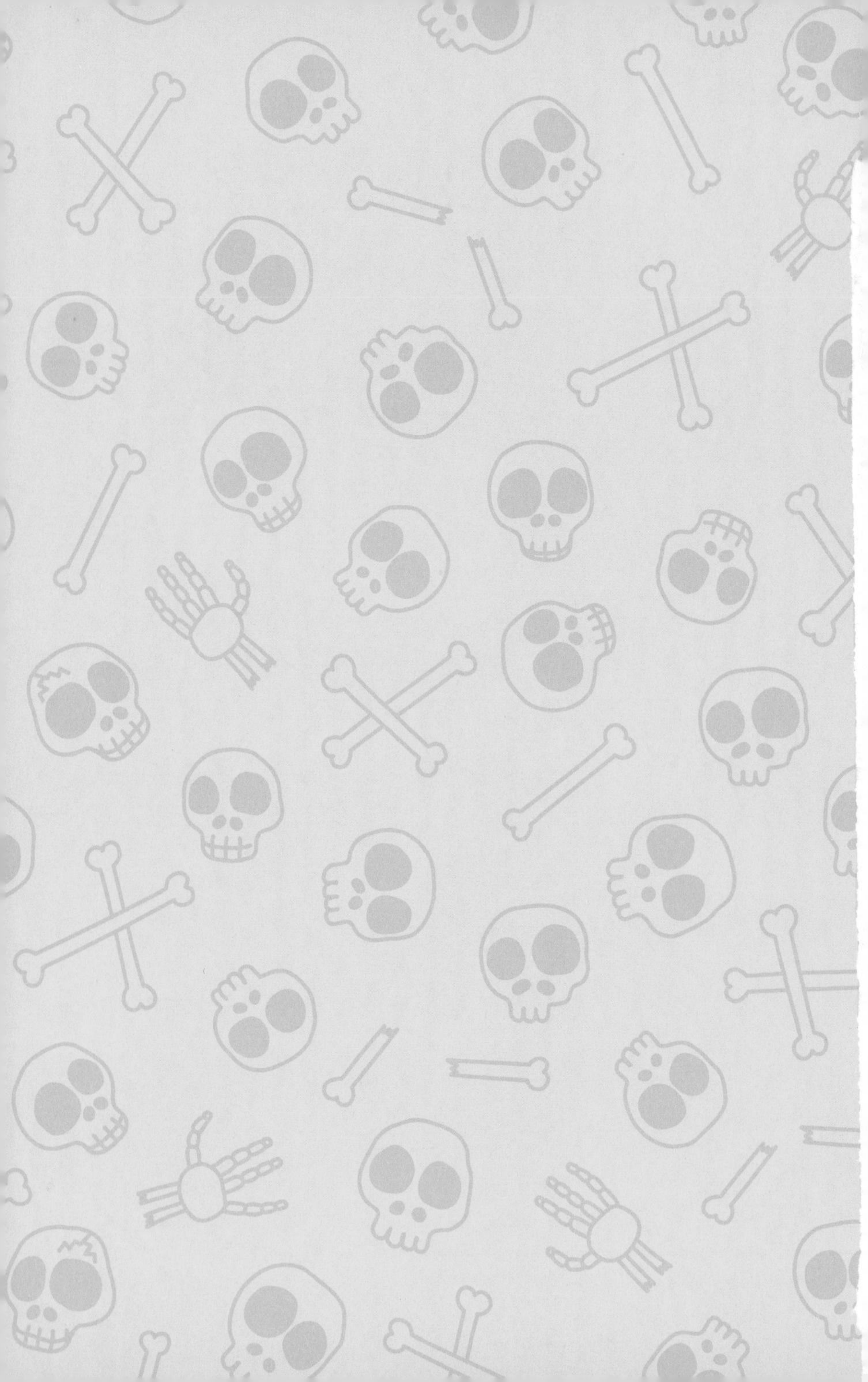

ALSO BY ROWLEY JEFFERSON

GREG HEFFLEY'S
DIARY OF A WIMPY KID BOOKS

Rowley Jefferson's Awesome Friendly SPOOKY STORIES

by Jeff Kinney

AMULET BOOKS

New York

Cataloging-in-Publication Data has been applied for and may be obtained from the Library of Congress.

ISBN 978-1-4197-5697-9

Cover design by Jeff Kinney, Marcie Lawrence, and Brenda E. Angelilli
Book design by Jeff Kinney

Printed and bound in the U.S.A.
10 9 8 7 6 5 4 3 2 1

Amulet Books are available at special discounts when purchased in quantity for premiums and promotions as well as fundraising or educational use. Special editions can also be created to specification. For details, contact specialsales@abramsbooks.com or the address below.

ABRAMS The Art of Books
195 Broadway, New York, NY 10007
abramsbooks.com

SPOOKY STORIES

READER BEWARE!

BOO! Did that scare you?

If it did maybe you should put this book down and pick something else that's a little less scary. There are some good books about unicorns and puppies and other happy things that you can read until you're ready for a book like this.

But if you like stories about skeletons and zombies and human heads, then crawl under the covers and turn the page.

And if you get too scared then you can always sleep in your parents' bed. But please don't tell them the reason you got spooked because I really don't want them to be mad at me.

I WARNED YOU!

The Changing

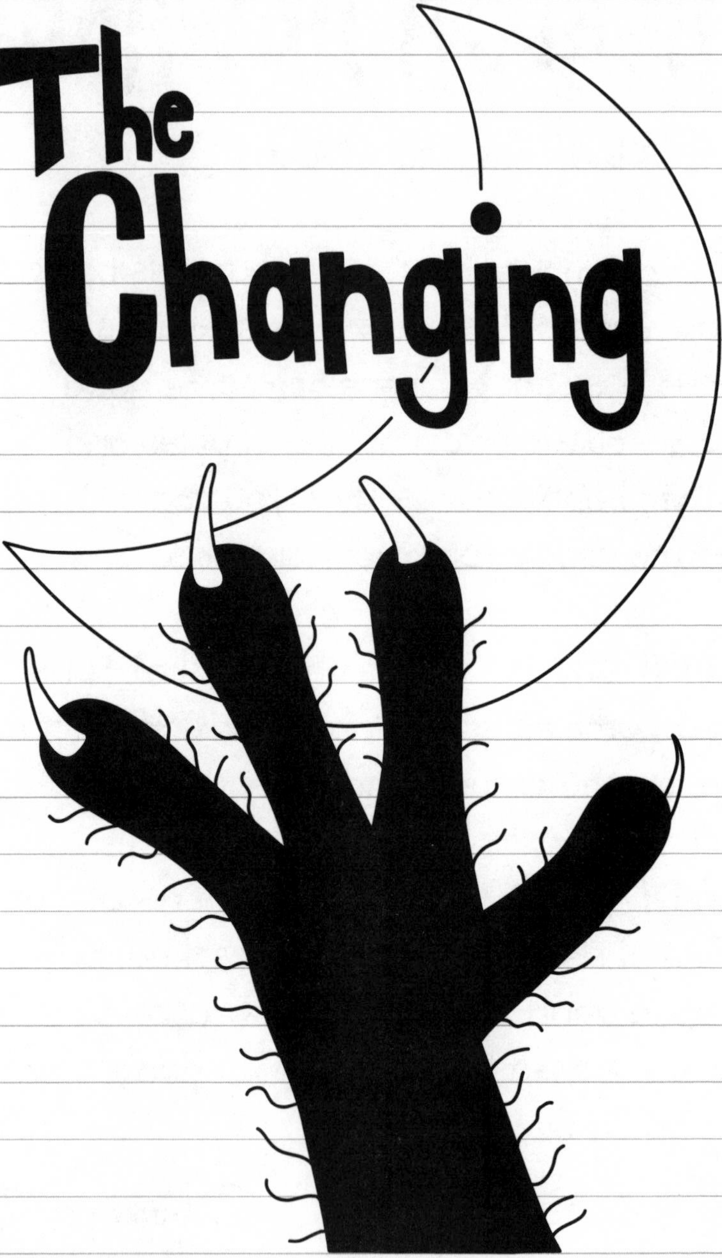

There once was a boy named Rowan, and Rowan was a happy child. He had two parents who loved him very much and he had lots of toys to play with.

Sometimes Rowan would bring his toys to school and play with them at recess, but he stopped doing that after he got bullied by some jerks.

That made Rowan sad because he thought playing with toys was the best thing about being a kid. But Rowan's classmates didn't feel the same way and they were always trying to act older than they really were.

One day when Rowan was in class he felt a strange tickling sensation under his armpit. He didn't know what it was so he asked his teacher Mrs. Pennington if he could please be excused to use the restroom.

When Rowan got to the bathroom he took off his shirt and was shocked to see a single hair growing from the center of his armpit.

Rowan didn't know what to do so he put his shirt back on and returned to class. And when he sat down he felt like everyone in the classroom could tell something was different about him, even Mrs. Pennington.

When the final bell rang, Rowan ran all the way home. He knew his mother kept some tweezers in the bathroom and he couldn't wait to use them to pull out that hair.

But when Rowan took his shirt off he could see it was too late for tweezers.

Suddenly hair started sprouting all OVER Rowan's body. And before long he was practically COVERED in it.

SPRONG

SPROING   BOING

By now Rowan was totally panicking. He went through his parents' bathroom cabinet to see if there was anything that might help and he found something he thought would do the trick.

But there's a reason kids shouldn't go poking around in their parents' bathroom cabinets. Because two seconds after Rowan opened the bottle he passed out from the fumes.

When Rowan woke up he was in his bed.
At first he thought maybe the whole
thing with the hair was just a bad dream
but one look at his arm told him it
wasn't.

Rowan's parents walked into his room
and he was afraid they were gonna be
mad at him for opening that bottle
of hair remover without asking. But
they didn't look mad at all. In fact, they
seemed kind of HAPPY.

Rowan's parents said they'd been waiting for this day for years and it was time for them to have the "Talk."

Rowan thought they had already had the Talk when his parents told him how babies were made. But they said this one was a totally different Talk.

His parents said that sometimes when a child turns a certain age their body starts to go through a "Changing." And that made Rowan sad because he liked himself just the way he was.

By now Rowan thought he knew where this was heading so he asked the question that had been on his mind all day.

Well that made Rowan's parents laugh and laugh. And Rowan felt embarrassed because it took them a long time to STOP laughing.

After Rowan's dad wiped the tears from his eyes he said Rowan was still a boy but he was a different KIND of boy. And when Rowan asked what he meant by that his dad gave him some bad news.

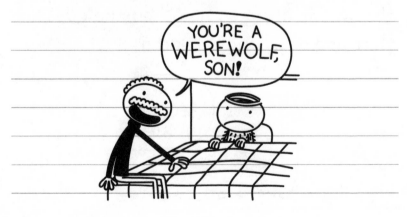

This was definitely NOT what Rowan wanted to hear. But when Rowan's mom saw the worried look on her son's face she said this was a day to CELEBRATE.

Rowan's parents told him he came from a long line of werewolves. And suddenly the pictures on the staircase wall made a lot more sense to Rowan.

Then Rowan's parents gave him some MORE bad news. They said THEY were both werewolves too.

Rowan started remembering clues growing up that should've told him his parents were werewolves. But he guessed deep down he didn't want to admit the truth.

Then Rowan started crying. He said he just wanted to be a regular kid and have a normal life.

But his parents said a werewolf could live a perfectly normal life as long as they kept on top of their grooming and hid who they really were from the rest of the world.

Rowan didn't WANT to hide who he was though. He had always been taught to be yourself and that's what he planned to do.

But Rowan's parents told him there are ignorant people in the world who don't like anyone who is different.

And Rowan knew exactly the type of
people his parents were talking about.

Then Rowan asked his parents a question
he wasn't sure he was ready to hear the
answer to.

BUT DON'T
WEREWOLVES
EAT PEOPLE?

Rowan's parents looked a little
uncomfortable and said that was a
subject for another Talk later on.

But Rowan had a feeling he knew the answer to his question so the next day he brought his toys with him to recess. And this time nobody dared to mess with him.

Rowan's example inspired his parents to stop hiding who THEY were too. And from that day on Rowan and his family lived as their true selves and everyone else just had to deal with it.

AROOOOOO!

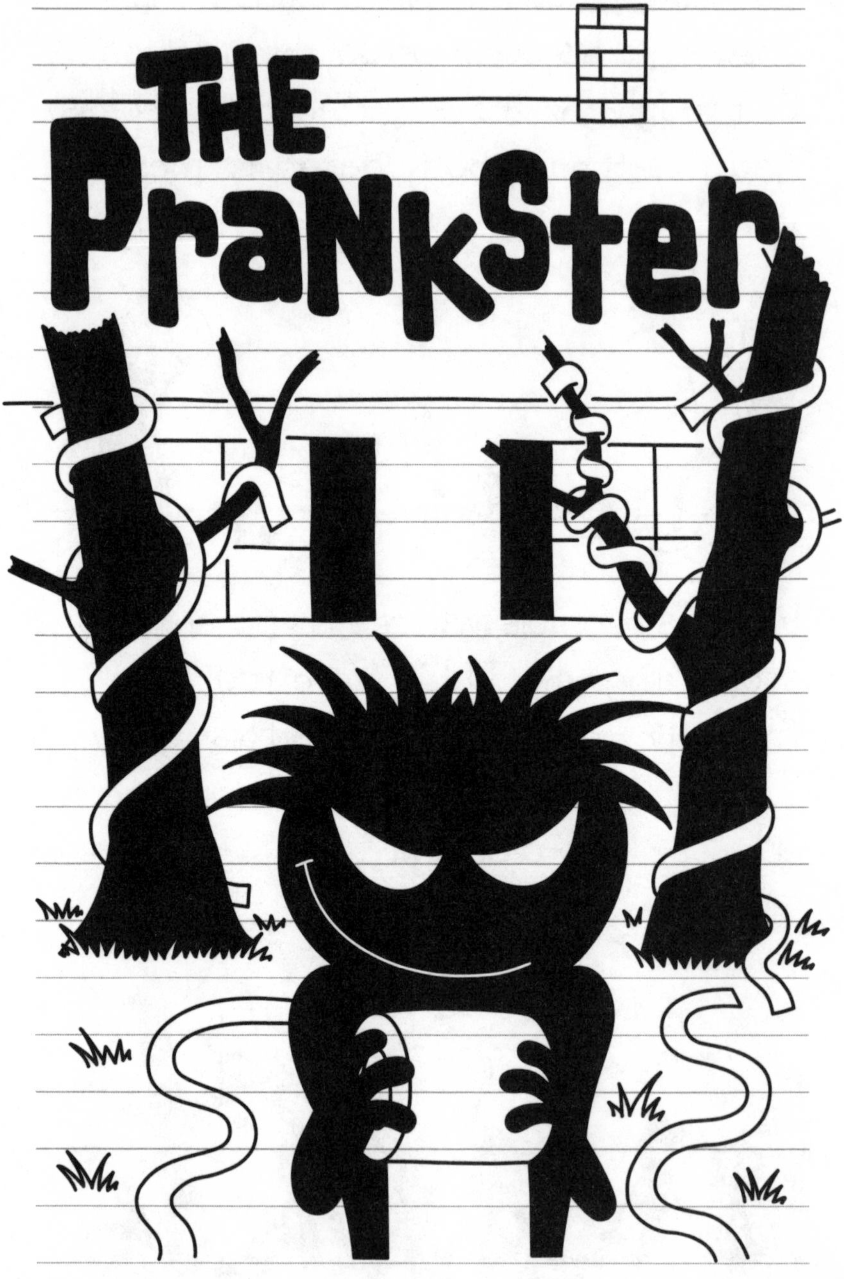
THE PRANKSTER

In a little seaside village somewhere in Europe there lived a man named Jasper. And everyone knew who Jasper was because he was the village prankster.

Most of Jasper's pranks were pretty harmless. One time he covered the baker's car in gift wrap, and another time he filled the village's only phone booth with popcorn.

17

Sometimes Jasper would even prank his own family members. And his mother never really forgave him for gluing all of her furniture to the ceiling.

But Jasper's most famous prank was the time he put the mayor's underwear up a flagpole, which everyone thought was pretty hilarious. Well everyone except the MAYOR.

That was the thing about Jasper's pranks. Most people thought they were pretty hilarious unless they were the one being pranked.

Anyway one morning Jasper woke up trying to figure out who he was gonna prank next. He couldn't decide if he wanted to toilet paper his next-door neighbor's house or replace the baker's cream-filled donuts with toothpaste.

The toilet paper thing felt like a lot of work and it had been a while since Jasper pranked Joris the baker so Jasper decided he'd go with the donut thing for today.

Jasper got out of bed and brushed his hair, then headed up the hill to the bakery. And on the way there he passed a few people he knew.

He waved to Marian the dressmaker and Miki the cheesemonger but neither one waved back. But he figured they were just sore at him for covering their shop windows in mustard the week before.

Things got stranger when Jasper walked into the bakery. His friend Dieter the shoemaker was walking out and when Jasper said hello, Dieter ignored him.

And a few seconds later when Marta the librarian walked in to buy her daily baguette she walked past Jasper like she didn't even see him.

When Marta went to the counter to buy her bread Joris was distracted and that's when Jasper made his move. He pulled the tube of toothpaste out of his pocket and grabbed the glass lid off the donut platter.

Or at least he TRIED to. Because when Jasper reached for the lid his hand went right THROUGH it.

Jasper was so confused that he ran outside and onto the street. But what happened next upset him even MORE. Because when he stood in front of the mirror shop he didn't have a REFLECTION.

Jasper realized that no one could see or hear him. And when he made a complete fool of himself nobody noticed.

Even when Jasper barged in on the Mommy and Me class at the yoga studio, everyone just kept doing their thing like he didn't exist.

Jasper tried talking himself into thinking this was a GOOD thing. Because if no one could see him he could pull off some really epic pranks.

Just then a line of people walked past Jasper. There was Brom, his best friend growing up, and his first school teacher, Mrs. Van Dijk. Everyone was dressed in black and looked really sad.

Then Jasper saw his own mother at the back of the line, bawling her eyes out.

Everyone was headed into the church, so Jasper followed them inside. And even though Jasper knew no one could see him he felt a little underdressed so he sat in the back pew by himself.

It didn't take long for Jasper to figure out that he was at a funeral. But he was still pretty shocked when he realized who the funeral was FOR.

The preacher said the guy who died was toilet papering somebody's front yard when he got struck by lightning. And you probably already figured out that person was JASPER.

So now Jasper knew the truth. He wasn't invisible all this time, he was DEAD. And he had to sit there while everyone came up to the front of the church to say a few words.

Usually at funerals people say NICE things about the person who died. But all anyone could talk about was Jasper's annoying pranks.

For the first time ever, Jasper could see that sometimes he took his pranks too far. And he wished he could live his whole life over again and become a fisherman or a librarian or just about anything other than the village prankster.

After the last person spoke it was time for final goodbyes. And when Jasper's mom went up to the casket it was a little hard for Jasper to watch.

Jasper had no idea what you're supposed to do at a funeral when you're the person who died. So even though it felt weird he went up to say his goodbyes too.

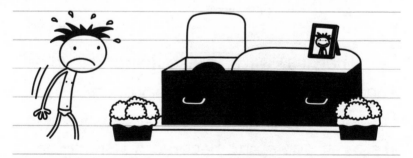

But there wasn't a body in the casket at ALL.

There was just a pumpkin with a face drawn on it which kind of looked like Jasper.

Then everyone started laughing at once. And that was the moment when Jasper realized he wasn't really dead and that this was all one big PRANK.

HA HA HA HEE HEE HEE HO HO

Jasper was happy he was alive but to be honest he was annoyed that the other villagers got him so good.

Besides he had a lot of QUESTIONS.

For one thing he couldn't figure out how his hand went through that glass donut lid at the bakery. Then Joris explained that his nephew was a whiz with technology and the whole donut platter was a hologram.

FSHRMM

And when Jasper asked why he couldn't see his reflection in the mirror the guy who owned the mirror shop said he'd replaced the mirrors with televisions that showed an empty sidewalk.

Then the people who were in the yoga studio said they almost lost it when Jasper walked in on their class.

It turned out the whole VILLAGE was in on the joke. And since pranking was kind of Jasper's thing he had a hard time admitting they got him.

Jasper told everyone it was a decent prank but his were way BETTER.

Then the preacher said this was actually a DOUBLE prank because the day before, a meteor wiped out the village and everyone in it.

That meant they were ALL dead and EVERYONE was a ghost.

Well this was the second time Jasper found out he was dead in one day, but this time he didn't take it as hard. Jasper always wanted to travel, and if he was a ghost he could fly wherever he wanted.

So he climbed to the top of the lighthouse and aimed himself toward Paris.

But it turns out the story about the meteor was a prank too. And this time the villagers thought maybe THEY were the ones who took a prank a little too far.

GHOST FRIEND

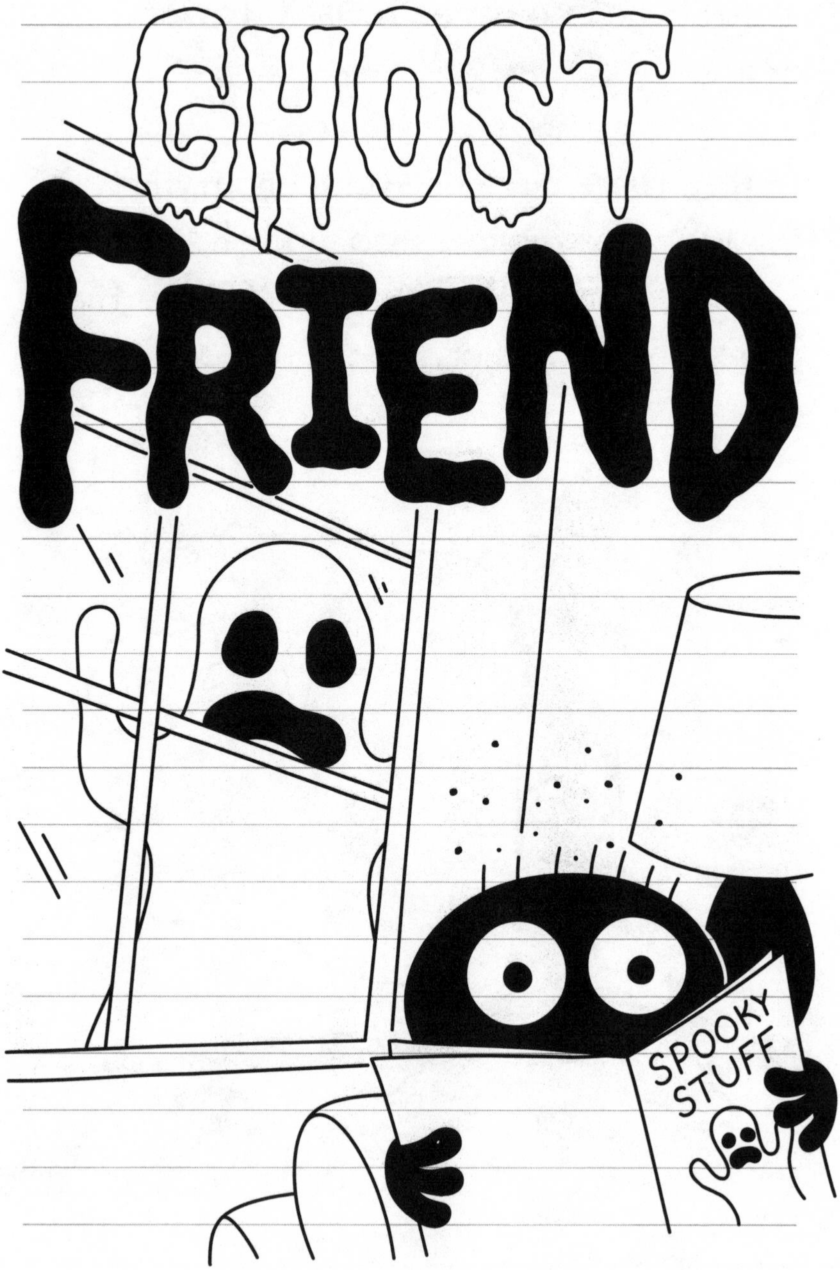

Rusty and Gabe were best friends from the time they were little. They hung out at Rusty's house every day after school, and on weekends they'd watch their favorite soccer team play on TV.

Most of the time Rusty and Gabe got along great but every once in a while Gabe did something that annoyed Rusty. But Rusty knew that even best friends can sometimes get on each other's nerves.

Then one day something terrible happened to Gabe. And I don't wanna get into the details because it's way too sad for a kid's book.

Later on that year Rusty was really sad because he missed his best friend. And even though Gabe did a lot of annoying things Rusty knew he would do anything to spend just one more afternoon with his pal.

Suddenly a cold gust of wind blew into Rusty's room and when he turned around there was his best friend Gabe.

Right now you are probably saying "Oh I guess Gabe wasn't dead after all!" but you're WRONG. Because this was the GHOST version of Gabe.

Gabe said he came back from the spirit world because he knew Rusty really needed him. And that kind of made Rusty feel bad for thinking about all the times Gabe annoyed him.

But Gabe said now that he was a ghost he wouldn't have to go home and they could hang out all night if they wanted.

Well Rusty was glad to have his friend back but the thing about staying up late made him a little nervous because this was a school night and he liked to get to bed early. But Rusty didn't say anything because he knew Gabe would tell him he was being a Goody Two-shoes.

Rusty said he should probably go downstairs and tell his parents that Gabe was back but Gabe said that would spoil their fun and they should keep this ghost thing a secret.

Gabe said they should just hang out and play video games like they did in the old days.

But when Rusty handed Gabe a controller it went right through his hands.

It turned out since Gabe was a ghost he couldn't touch anything. So he had Rusty play the game FOR him which wasn't really that much fun for Rusty.

After a few hours Rusty said he needed to do his homework.

Gabe said he was glad HE didn't have to
do homework anymore since he was dead.
And he kept talking which made it really
hard for Rusty to concentrate.

Finally Rusty put a soccer game on TV
so Gabe would stop bugging him for a
while. But Gabe booed the whole time, and
Rusty couldn't tell if that was because
Gabe didn't like one of the teams or if he
was just making ghost noises.

After a while Gabe got bored with the
game and he started trying out his
ghost powers like walking through walls.
And that made it even harder for Rusty
to concentrate on his homework.

YO! CHECK
THIS OUT!

Rusty gave up on his homework and told
Gabe he needed to go to sleep. But Gabe
said that was kind of inconvenient for
HIM because ghosts don't sleep.

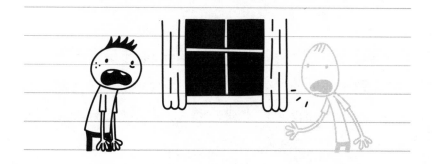

Rusty got ready for bed and hoped Gabe would just float away to wherever it is that ghosts go at night. But even after Rusty got under the covers and turned off the lights Gabe kept hanging around talking.

And all Gabe wanted to do was talk about this girl named Kelsey Reed who he had a crush on.

Somehow Rusty fell asleep and when he woke up Gabe was STILL talking. And he kept right on talking while Rusty got ready for school.

Rusty told Gabe he'd catch up with him when he got back from school. But Gabe said it would be too boring to wait in Rusty's bedroom all day so he was coming WITH him.

It turns out Rusty was the only one who could see or hear Gabe, and he talked the whole way to school. But Rusty didn't really respond because he didn't want anyone thinking he was talking to himself.

First period for Rusty was Science. And unfortunately Marcus Meeks was absent so that meant there was an empty seat right behind Rusty.

The next period was Spanish and there was a pop quiz. Rusty didn't get a chance to look over his notes the night before so he knew he was in trouble. But this was where having a ghost friend came in handy for Rusty.

Rusty's teacher graded the quizzes during class. And when Rusty got his quiz back he remembered that Gabe had always been lousy in Spanish.

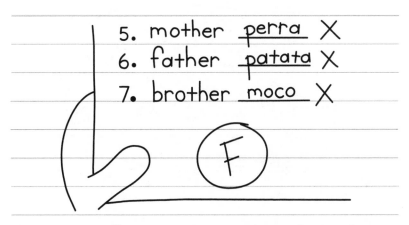

5. mother   perra   X
6. father   patata   X
7. brother   moco   X

F

At recess, Rusty was too tired to play kickball with the other kids so he sat on the bench. Then Kelsey Reed sat down next to him.

Kelsey started talking to Rusty and she was really nice. But when Rusty tried to talk he could barely think because Gabe was being really annoying.

On the walk home all Gabe could talk about was Kelsey Reed. And this time Rusty didn't even bother responding.

That night Rusty needed to study for
a test but of course Gabe made that
impossible.

By now Rusty was overtired and cranky
and finally he just SNAPPED.

Rusty blamed Gabe for his bad grade in
Spanish and said his constant talking was
driving him nuts. And he said maybe it
would've been better if Gabe hadn't come
back in the FIRST place.

But as soon as the words left Rusty's mouth he wished he could take them back because he could tell he'd hurt his friend's feelings.

SNIFF

Gabe said that if Rusty felt that way then maybe he should just go back to the spirit world. And that kind of got Rusty a little teary-eyed because he knew if Gabe was gone for good he'd probably start missing him again.

Rusty said he was sorry and that he didn't want Gabe to go to the spirit world.

So Gabe stuck around, and it wasn't for a little while either. Rusty's grades went downhill and he didn't bother going to college because he knew he'd never get any work done with Gabe in the picture. Plus he never got a girlfriend because he knew Gabe would probably mess that up too.

And even though Rusty thought it was nice to have his best friend around, sometimes he wondered if he'd made a terrible mistake.

THE BITER

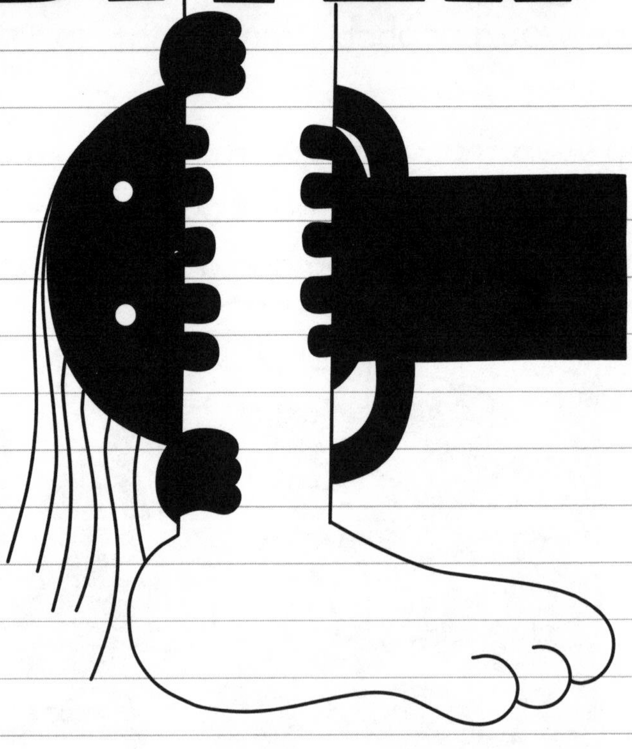

Once there was a girl named Lilli. And from the time she was a baby, Lilli liked putting things in her mouth.

Right now you're probably saying "ALL babies like putting things in their mouths." But trust me this kid was DIFFERENT.

It wasn't just baby toys, it was EVERYTHING. So Lilli's parents had to get used to their stuff being covered in baby drool all the time.

Lilli's pediatrician told her parents their baby was teething and that's why she always needed something to chew on.

So Lilli's parents just tried to ignore her and let Lilli do her thing. But then Lilli's teeth started coming in and they were SHARP.

Lilli's parents kept hoping she'd grow out of this stage but she never did.

When Lilli got a little older her parents tried to set up playdates with other kids, but they always ended in tears.

Lilli's parents bought a bunch of books to help teach their daughter that biting was bad but the lesson never seemed to sink in. Plus books were some of Lilli's favorite things to chew on.

IT'S NOT *Polite* TO **BITE**

By the time Lilli was old enough to go to full-day kindergarten she didn't have many friends. Her parents were kind of nervous sending her to school because of her biting issue but they thought maybe Lilli's teacher could figure out how to handle it better than they could.

But they probably should've given her teacher a heads-up about Lilli when they dropped her off for school.

So Lilli got sent home early on her first day of kindergarten. And this was a big problem for her parents because they both worked from home so they couldn't be watching her every second.

They took her back to the pediatrician to see if there was anything she could do. The doctor ran some tests and a few days later she called them in to share the results.

It turns out the reason Lilli liked biting things so much was because she was a VAMPIRE. And even though it was hard for Lilli's parents to hear that, they were glad they finally had some answers.

The doctor said the good news was that vampires aren't contagious until they're full-grown, so right now the biting was more annoying than anything.

Lilli's parents didn't understand how their daughter was a vampire since neither of THEM were vampires.

But then Lilli's mom remembered that when she was pregnant she got bitten by a vampire bat so that must've been how it happened.

Lilli's parents were happy to know what was going on with their daughter but it still didn't solve their problem. They really needed her to be in school but they couldn't send her if she was gonna keep biting people.

Lilli's pediatrician said there was a special school where Lilli could learn with other kids just like her. But even though the brochure looked nice, Lilli's parents knew they could never afford to send her to a place like that.

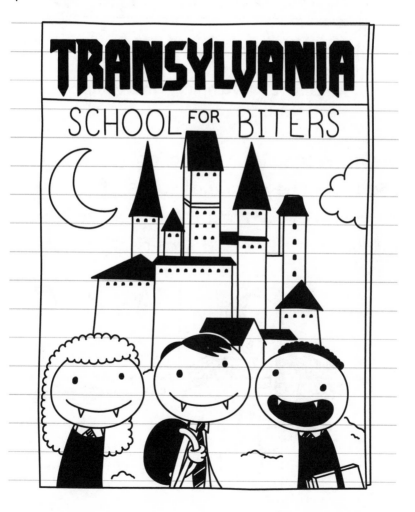

Lilli's parents asked her pediatrician if there was anything else she could do for their daughter. So the doctor wrote a note to Lilli's school explaining the situation.

FROM THE DESK OF NISHA SAAD, MD

Dear Principal Septian,

Lilli is a vampire, and vampires need to bite.

Well it turned out the school was GREAT about it. They made all sorts of changes in the classroom and from then on when Lilli bit her teacher it was really no big deal.

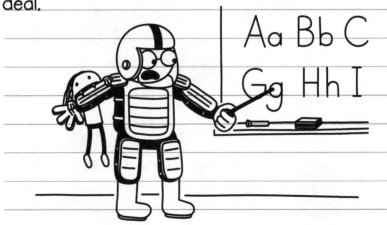

Aa Bb C
Gg Hh I

They even made changes in the cafeteria so Lilli could feel included.

Lilli's classmates thought being a vampire was cool so now everybody wanted to be her friend. And they all wanted to be just like her so they started ACTING like her too.

Things were going pretty great for Lilli at school and she had a ton of new friends. And now EVERYONE wanted to come over for playdates.

But then one day the pediatrician called and asked Lilli's parents to come back into her office. She said she had read the test results wrong and that Lilli wasn't a vampire after all. She was just a bad kid who liked biting people.

Well you would think that Lilli's parents would be thrilled to find out that their daughter wasn't a vampire.

But Lilli was doing great at school and they really didn't want her home during the workday.

So they decided to keep the test results to themselves. And when Lilli had a birthday party and everyone in her class came, her parents felt like they'd made the right choice.

THE HUMAN HEAD

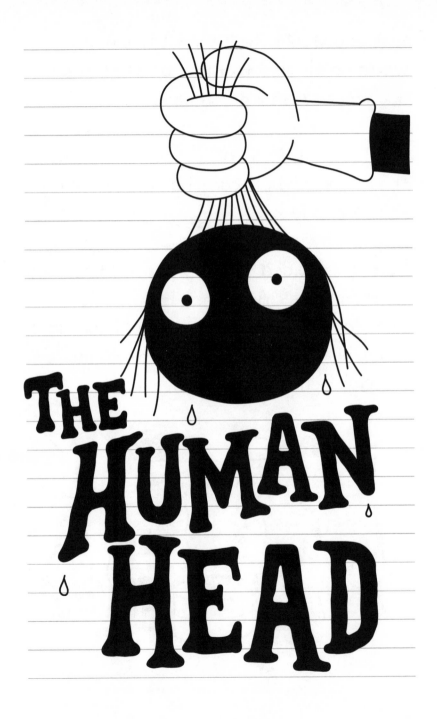

Everybody's heard the legend of the Headless Horseman who terrorized the town of Sleepy Hollow a long time ago.

But I'll bet you've never heard the story of the Human Head who lived a few miles away in the town of Elmsford. And just because the Human Head didn't go around chucking flaming jack-o'-lanterns at people doesn't mean his story isn't worth telling too.

63

So let's start at the beginning. Before the Human Head of Elmsford got his nickname he was just a regular kid named Anders.

Anders was normal in every way except he was born without a body. But that didn't stop Anders from doing all the things other kids his age did.

Anders's parents loved him very much and told him he could be whatever he wanted to be. And that made Anders feel good.

Anders had lots of friends in elementary school and was so popular that he got voted class president in the fifth grade.

VOTE FOR ANDERS

HEAD AND SHOULDERS ABOVE THE REST

But things changed when it came time for Anders to go to middle school. A few of his closest friends moved away during the summer and some others went to private school. So when September came around, Anders felt like he was starting over.

The first day of middle school isn't easy for anyone but it's even harder when you're a late bloomer like Anders and you haven't hit your growth spurt yet.

Back in elementary school, Anders stayed in one classroom the whole day. But middle school was a different thing and sometimes Anders had trouble getting from one class to another before the bell rang.

When lunchtime came, Anders was happy because he really needed a break and plus his mom had packed him a bologna sandwich and his favorite snack. But by the time he got to the cafeteria all the good seats were already taken.

Anders spotted a table across the cafeteria with a bunch of empty seats. And that's where Anders saw the Headless Horseman for the first time.

Right now you're probably thinking "Oh no the Headless Horseman is gonna do something terrible to Anders!" but don't worry because this was way before the Headless Horseman turned evil. In fact this was way before he got that nickname and a few years before he even learned to ride a horse.

For now the Headless Horseman just went by his real name which was Gunther. And like I said he wasn't evil yet so when he spotted Anders he invited him to sit at his table.

Well from the moment they met, Anders and Gunther became fast friends.

Gunther didn't mind that Anders was a little chatty and Anders didn't mind that Gunther shoveled food down his neck hole to eat.

The two boys started hanging out after school almost every day. Anders helped Gunther with his homework and Gunther helped Anders with just about everything else.

Fall turned to winter and the two best friends made lots of happy memories together.

PLOP

When February rolled around, everyone at school was buzzing about the big Valentine's Dance.

VALENTINE'S DANCE

February 14th • 7:00-9:00 p.m.

But both boys were too shy to ask anyone to go with them and before long it seemed like everyone at school was paired up.

Gunther and Anders were sad because they knew they'd be spending the night of the dance playing video games like they always did.

But something happened the week before Valentine's Day that changed everything.

A girl named Prudence whose family had just moved to town showed up at the school, and she was so pretty that some of the guys who'd asked other girls to the dance were kind of kicking themselves.

Even though Gunther and Anders both thought Prudence was cute neither one of them was brave enough to ask her to the Valentine's Dance. But then Anders had an idea.

He said maybe if the two of them teamed up they could convince Prudence to go to the dance with them. And after a lot of rehearsing in front of the mirror they felt like this might actually WORK.

The next day the guys brought a bouquet of flowers to school and got the courage to ask Prudence to the dance. And believe it or not she said YES.

BLUSH

On the night of the big dance Anders put
on some of his dad's cologne so he'd smell
good for his date. And Gunther's parents
rented him a cape so he'd look extra
handsome.

So when the guys showed up at
Prudence's house they were looking
pretty sharp.

When the three kids got to the school
they didn't know what to expect because
this was the first time any of them had
been to a real dance.

But the Party Planning Committee had really done their job because the cafeteria looked totally AMAZING.

Anders, Gunther, and Prudence hung out by the refreshments table for a while and Anders told a few jokes he had been practicing. And when Prudence laughed, Anders thought things couldn't be going any better.

When the music really got cranking no one wanted to be the first to step onto the dance floor. But then Gunther surprised everyone by totally going for it.

It turns out Gunther was a really awesome dancer. And no one was happier about that than ANDERS.

That was all it took to get everyone
ELSE out on the dance floor. And before
long the party was in high gear.

Anders and Gunther started a conga
line and everyone joined in. But Anders
wasn't looking where he was going and
that led to disaster.

Prudence was kind of upset because until now she thought Gunther and Anders were one person.

She was a little sore at the guys for not being honest with her about who they really were. But after Anders apologized she forgave them, and when a slow song came on, Gunther asked her to dance.

Even though Anders had a great spot right next to the cookie platter, the rest of the night wasn't very much fun for him.

After that night, things started to change between Anders and Gunther. Both of them liked Prudence, and at school they fought for her attention.

But Prudence liked both guys for different reasons. So on Friday nights she'd go roller-skating with Gunther and on Saturdays she'd go with Anders to a museum or a foreign-language film.

Even though Anders really enjoyed
spending time with Prudence he missed
hanging out with his pal even more. So
one day at lunch Anders told Gunther
that if he was in love with Prudence then
Anders wouldn't get in his way.

That night Gunther went to Prudence's
house with a bouquet of flowers to
declare his love for her. But Prudence
said her heart belonged to somebody else,
and Gunther left brokenhearted.

And you can probably guess who Prudence chose instead.

Gunther never got over his heartbreak. And when he grew up he became the legendary Headless Horseman who terrorized young couples on Valentine's Day and not on Halloween night like everyone always thinks.

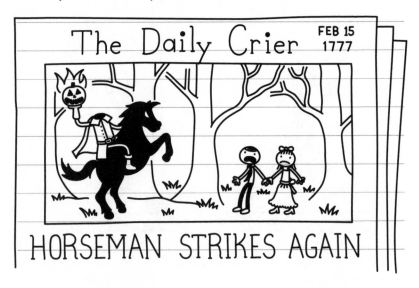

Believe it or not Anders and Prudence dated all the way through high school. They took a break when they went to colleges in different states but got back together after they graduated.

Prudence became a veterinarian and Anders became an accountant, and they raised their family in Elmsford. And even though Prudence and Anders never made the front page of the newspaper like their famous friend, they did make a difference in the town where they lived.

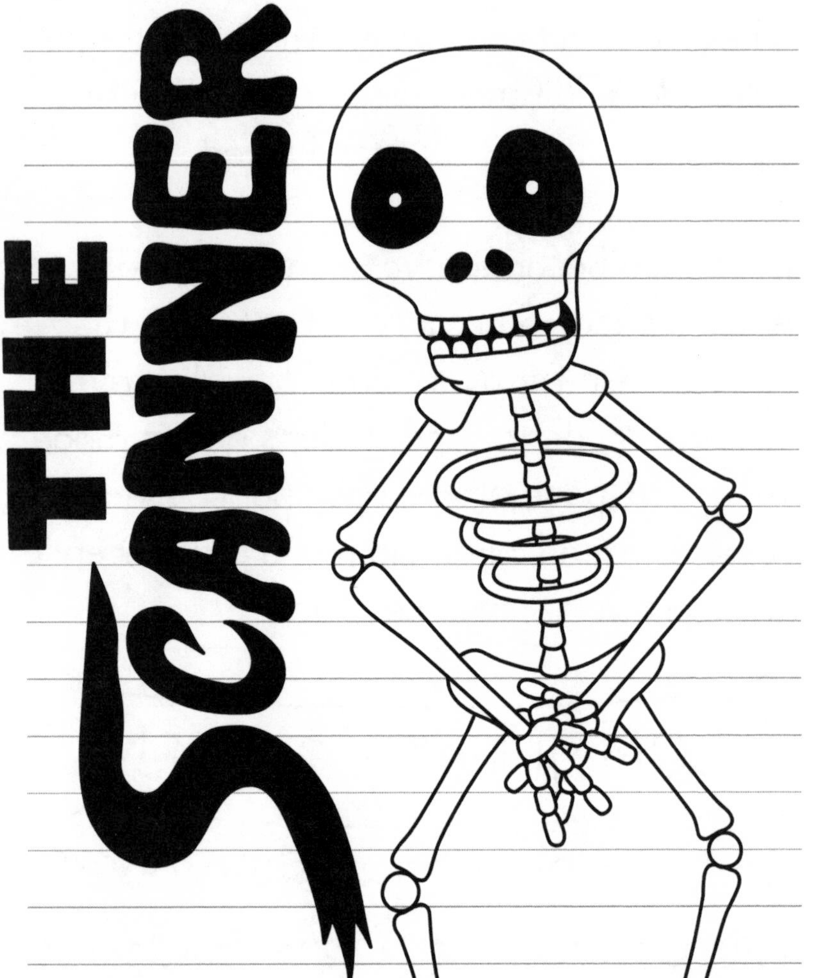
THE SCANNER

Today was a big day at the international airport because it was the unveiling of the brand-new high tech security scanner. The new machine could scan a bunch of people at once and that meant shorter lines at the airport, which everyone was pretty jazzed about.

CRUISE THROUGH SECURITY!

Everybody knew this was a big deal so tons of people showed up hoping to be the first ones to go through the scanner.

But the scientists who made the machine were under a lot of pressure to get it done quickly and they didn't really have time to test it out.

So everyone was pretty surprised when the first batch of people went through the machine and they came out the other side as SKELETONS.

Right now you are probably saying "It's so sad those people died going through the scanner" but don't worry because somehow they were still ALIVE. And the scientists who made the machine couldn't figure out HOW.

At first the people who went through the scanner were kind of annoyed they got turned into skeletons.

But they felt better about things when they became celebrities overnight.

People realized that if they were skeletons they didn't need to spend all their money on skin cream and makeup and clothes and stuff like that. So now EVERYONE wanted to go through the scanner, and the next day the airport was totally PACKED.

It turns out there were a LOT of good things about being a skeleton.

People figured out that they could sleep in late because they didn't have to take a shower. And since they didn't have stomachs they started sleeping EXTRA late because they didn't need to eat breakfast either.

CLATTER
CLATTER

Since no one had any muscles nobody needed to exercise. And if they broke a bone, all it took was a little duct tape to fix things up.

A bunch of other annoying things also went away, like pimples and warts and skinned knees and bedhead. And emojis got a lot simpler too.

Another nice thing was that everyone could use the same restrooms since no one really needed privacy anymore.

Everyone looked the same so people were a lot nicer to each other too. And the more people who went through the scanner, the better things seemed to get.

But before long people started noticing some things that WEREN'T so great. A lot of businesses closed because nobody needed their services anymore.

Halloween was a lot more boring because everyone just went as the same thing.

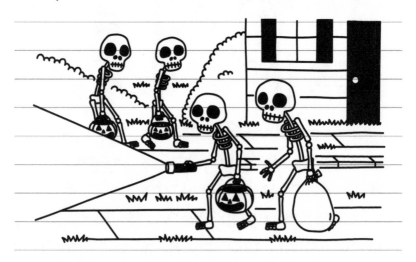

Parents kept picking up the wrong kids from daycare and after a while it was a total MESS.

And even though it was great that everyone looked the same, people started to miss the old days when they DIDN'T.

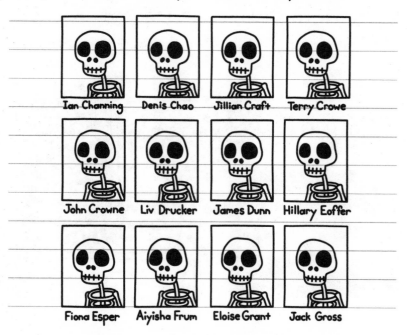

Ian Channing   Denis Chao   Jillian Craft   Terry Crowe

John Crowne   Liv Drucker   James Dunn   Hillary Eoffer

Fiona Esper   Aiyisha Frum   Eloise Grant   Jack Gross

In fact people started missing a LOT of things, like having lips and eyeballs and not being so cold all the time. And everyone realized they'd made a terrible mistake and wanted to change BACK.

But the scientists who built the scanner never figured out why it worked to begin with. So they had no idea how to make the thing go in REVERSE.

Well this made the people who got turned into skeletons MAD. And on a cold winter's night they stormed the airport.

The skeletons dragged the scanner out of the building and threw it down the nearest cliff, where it blew up.

Then the craziest thing happened. The skeletons all turned back into how they were before, minus their clothes. And everyone was glad they were back to normal but they wished they had done this on a warmer night.

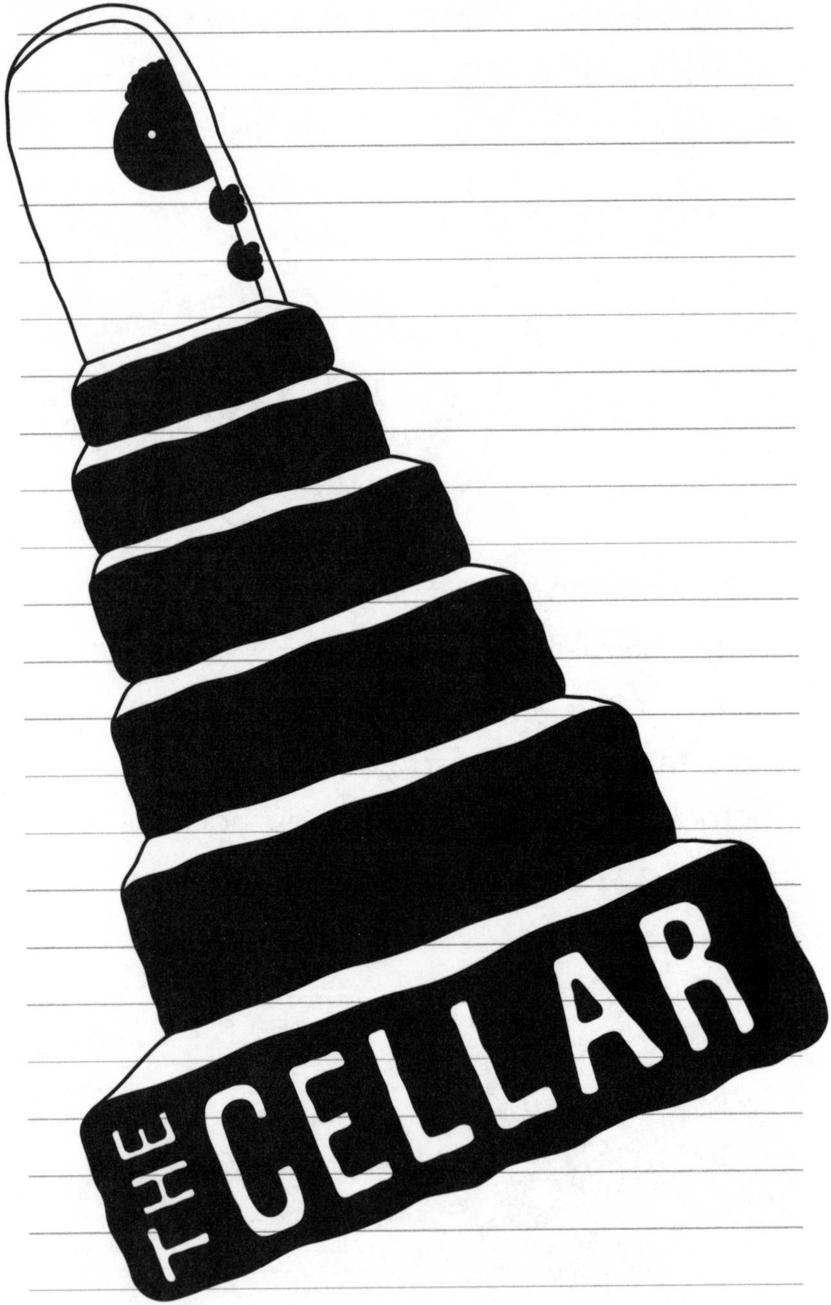
THE CELLAR

Long ago there was a boy named Rafe, and Rafe was a very happy boy. He lived in a hut made from mud and straw with his parents. And even though they didn't have much, they were happy to have each other.

Rafe's parents were very proud of their boy. He was growing up strong and healthy and he never once complained about cleaning out the chicken coop.

Rafe would wake up at the crack of dawn and go to bed when the sun went down. And on special nights Rafe's parents gave him a candle so he could stay up a little longer to read.

Sometimes if Rafe was enjoying a book he'd stay up EXTRA late and read under the covers. But it turns out that wasn't such a good idea back then.

Rafe's favorite stories were the ones about other children, because Rafe didn't have any friends of his own. In fact Rafe had never met ANYONE besides his mom and dad.

Sometimes Rafe would ask his parents if they could take a trip to a place where there were other people. But Rafe's parents said the journey would be too dangerous and they showed him why.

So Rafe made pretend friends out of mud and straw to play with, which was OK but Rafe really wished he had the real thing.

One night after Rafe finished reading he went into the kitchen to get some water. But then he heard strange noises unlike anything he'd heard before.

The sounds were coming from the cellar. And even though Rafe was very curious about the noises, his parents had told him he must never, ever go down in the cellar.

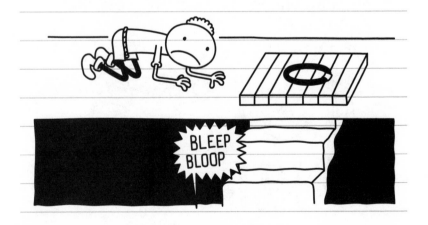

The next morning at breakfast Rafe described the mysterious sounds he heard the night before.

But his parents said maybe Rafe had been dreaming because he was making nonsense noises.

Rafe wanted to ask his parents what was in the cellar and why his dad was down there every Monday through Friday from 9:00 a.m. until 5:00 p.m. But he knew they didn't like to talk about those things.

Years passed and Rafe didn't hear the sounds again.

By now Rafe was eighteen years old and was almost as tall as his father. Rafe's parents could see that their boy had become a man and they said it was time to tell him the truth about where they came from.

So they described a world with "cars" and "airplanes" and "medicine" and other things that made Rafe's head spin.

They told Rafe the world they came from was wonderful in some ways but there was a dark side too. Then they told him about the glowing objects called "screens" that had everyone under their spell.

They explained that when Rafe was born they didn't want him to grow up under the spell of screens. So they made a decision to leave their world behind.

All of a sudden everything made sense
to Rafe. His parents were TIME
TRAVELERS, and they took him back to
a simpler time to PROTECT him.

But when Rafe mentioned the time-
travel thing his parents had a pretty
good chuckle and told him he had it all
wrong.

They said when they left their world
behind they meant they just moved
away from the city and PRETENDED
they were living in the dark ages.

Then Rafe's dad said he had something
he'd been waiting a long time to show him.

So he opened the cellar door and took Rafe down the steps, where Rafe saw things that totally blew his mind, like a computer and a printer and a fancy chair on wheels.

Rafe's dad said he had a job where he worked from home, and then he introduced Rafe to his co-workers.

HIIII RAFE!

Rafe started to feel dizzy and said he needed to sit down. So he sat in his dad's chair which was a LOT more comfortable than the crummy stools he was used to.

Rafe's parents could see that their son wasn't happy and they felt kind of bad for lying to him all his life. And they thought maybe they'd gone a little overboard trying to protect him from the modern world.

Then Rafe's dad got an idea for how to make it up to his son. He told Rafe that now that he was a grown man there was something he should have. And he gave Rafe his very first phone.

Rafe's parents said that there was one more secret they needed to tell him. They said they weren't surrounded by sharks and wolves and snakes and that they were only a few miles from a big city. Then they said it was time for Rafe to join the modern world and get a job and start a family of his own.

But now that Rafe had a phone he wasn't interested in anything else, and he didn't see any reason to ever leave home. So Rafe's parents thought maybe they'd had the right idea to begin with.

THE NAP

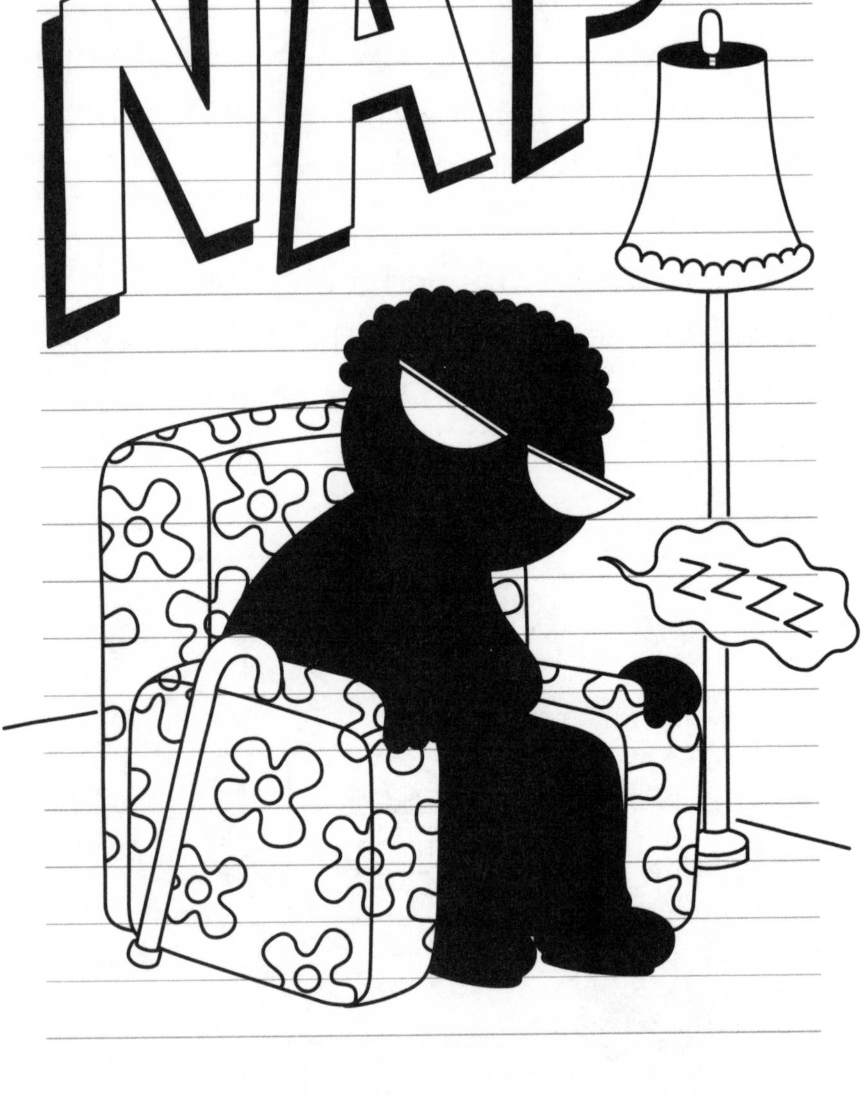
ZZZZ

There once was a woman who lived in a retirement community all by herself and her name was Frances. But everyone in her family called her Great Aunt Fannie or just Fannie for short.

Speaking of her family, Fannie didn't have any kids but she had lots of nieces and nephews and they had kids of their own. But none of them ever came to visit Fannie because they were too wrapped up in their own lives to visit her.

Fannie lived in a little condo but she had a really big TV. She needed a big TV because her eyesight wasn't that great and the only thing that really made her happy was watching her soap operas.

Every day Fannie would do the same thing. She'd watch her programs until she got tired and then she'd take a nap in her comfy chair. And when she was done with her nap she'd make herself a sandwich and watch more soap operas until the news came on.

One day while she was watching her programs she saw an ad for something she thought might be useful for a person like her.

It was this little gadget with a button on it that you could press if you ever fell and needed help.

Fannie thought that might be a good thing to have since she lived alone. So she called the number on the screen and placed an order, which was the first time she'd ever spent money on something like that.

In fact the only thing Fannie ever did with her money was write checks for her nieces and nephews and their kids on their birthdays.

And even though Fannie was never late
with a birthday card she never got a
thank-you from anyone except for her
six-year-old great niece Amber, who was
the only one in the family who wasn't
rotten.

On the weekends, Fannie's routine was a
little different because her soap operas
weren't on TV on those days. So she'd
usually have a big lunch and then take an
extra-long nap afterward.

One Saturday everyone in town was all
excited because it was the day of the Big
Game.

And since the tickets to the Big Game were sold out most people had to watch it on TV.

Well no one in Fannie's family had a big TV but they knew someone who DID. So a few hours before the Big Game, Gary Mack and a bunch of the guys piled into his pickup truck and headed to Great Aunt Fannie's retirement community.

But when they got to Fannie's condo and knocked on the door no one answered. So Little Dougie turned the doorknob and it was unlocked.

Aunt Fannie was asleep in her comfy chair in front of the TV. And when they saw her sitting there with her head tilted forward they thought she was DEAD.

The guys were all pretty sad because Fannie was their oldest relative and also because she was always on time with those birthday checks. But they didn't have a lot of time for tears because the Big Game was only a few hours away.

So Gary Mack made a few calls and found a funeral home that could move things along that afternoon.

It turned out the people at the funeral home wanted to watch the Big Game too. So after a quick service everyone was out of there.

You might be thinking "Oh no Great Aunt Fannie got buried alive!" But you probably forgot that Fannie ordered that electronic gadget and when she woke up she just pressed the button to call for help.

Well that thing worked just as good
as they said it did on the commercial
and help arrived a few minutes later.
And luckily the guys from the company
figured out what happened pretty quick.

After they got Fannie out of the
ground they gave her a ride back to her
retirement community.

And when Fannie opened the door to her
condo she was pretty surprised by what
she found.

Gary Mack and the other guys were happy to see Fannie alive but they were also a little distracted because the Big Game was on and the score was really close. Gary Mack didn't want to give up his seat in the comfy chair in front of the TV so Fannie had to sit on the couch with the other guys.

GOALLL!

After the Big Game was over everyone told Fannie they sure were glad she was alive but then they went home and left a huge mess for her to clean up on her own.

After that day things pretty much went back to normal, except Fannie started putting a little less money in everyone's birthday cards.

Fannie also started locking the door to her condo before she sat down for her afternoon naps because she really didn't want a repeat of what happened before.

And just to make DOUBLE sure she didn't get buried alive again she cut a ping-pong ball in half and drew a dot on each side so she could look like she was awake even when she wasn't.

A few months later Amber found out what happened to Great Aunt Fannie on the day of the Big Game, and she felt terrible about it. So she came to visit Fannie at her condo.

Fannie and Amber had a ball making cookies and they promised they'd do it again soon.

From that day on every time the family had a get-together Amber made sure Fannie was invited. And those were some of the happiest days of Fannie's life.

Gary Mack's family even invited her to join them on their summer vacation and she was really excited about that.

So this story kind of has a happy ending because Fannie's good-for-nothing family turned themselves around before it was too late. And it was all because of the kindness of a six-year-old girl.

But this story has a sad ending too because right before the start of the summer vacation Great Aunt Fannie passed away and no one even noticed until the week was halfway over.

THE STAIN

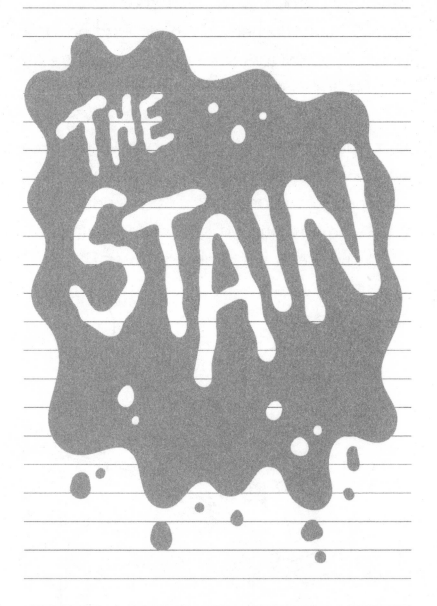

One Saturday afternoon Robbie's parents asked him if he'd like to go to the mall. Robbie was very excited because going to the mall was a special treat, and on the car ride Robbie thought of all the fun he'd have once he got there.

But Robbie's parents weren't at the mall to have fun, they were there to SHOP. And they visited the types of stores only grown-ups like.

Robbie's parents could see that their son wasn't having very much fun. So Robbie's dad gave him five dollars and told him he could go buy himself an ice cream. And his dad told Robbie that was enough money for TWO cones so Robbie should get him one too.

Robbie felt very proud that his parents trusted him and he told them he'd be right back.

For Robbie this was a very big deal. Even though the ice cream shop was just a few doors down this was the first time he'd been apart from his parents in such a crowded place.

Robbie walked out of the store and into the concourse which was packed with strangers. He clutched the money his dad gave him very tightly because he didn't want to drop it.

Then Robbie spotted his favorite ride which was a rocket ship that went back and forth. But Robbie reminded himself that he was too old for kiddie rides now and he clutched his five dollars even tighter to make sure he didn't spend it.

WHEEEE!

Robbie made it to the ice cream shop and was proud of himself for getting that far on his own. But when he got to the front counter he didn't know what to do because there were a lot of flavors and it was so hard to choose.

TE	CHOCOLATE	RAINBOW SHERBET	MINT CHOCOLATE CHIP	LEMON
SE CKS	VANILLA	STRAWBERRY	COFFEE	BIRT CA
TE P	PISTACHIO		COOKIE DOUGH	ROCK ROA

Robbie's two favorite ice cream flavors were rocky road and strawberry. So Robbie got rocky road for himself and strawberry for his dad because he knew his dad would probably share with him.

On his way back to the store where his parents were shopping Robbie saw that rocket ship again. Robbie had just enough money left over for one ride but he wanted to show his parents he could be responsible and bring back their change.

So he closed his eyes when he walked by the ride. But that was a bad idea because he tripped and his rocky road ice cream ended up on the ground.

TRIP

Robbie was so upset he almost cried.
He tried to put his ice cream cone back
together again but it was hopeless.

SMOOSH

After Robbie cleaned up his mess he
went to the store where his parents
were shopping. His dad's strawberry ice
cream was starting to melt but Robbie
was still hoping his dad would share some
with him.

Then Robbie had an idea. And it wasn't
the kind of idea Robbie USUALLY had.

He decided to pretend that the strawberry ice cream cone was HIS and the one he dropped was his DAD's. And this was a really big deal because Robbie had never told a fib in his whole life.

Robbie was so nervous lying to his parents that he almost cried again. And he felt terrible when his parents actually BELIEVED him.

But Robbie's dad said it was OK because he wasn't that hungry anyway. And that made Robbie feel even WORSE because he knew his dad was just being nice.

In fact he felt so bad he could barely enjoy his strawberry ice cream on the ride home.

When Robbie got back to his room his stomach didn't feel that good. And he couldn't tell if it was because of the ice cream or the fib he'd told his parents.

Then Robbie noticed a small pink spot on his white shirt. And he realized he must've gotten some strawberry ice cream on it.

Robbie knew his parents wouldn't be happy with him for getting ice cream on his crisp white shirt. So he went into the bathroom to try and scrub it clean before they found out.

But the spot was growing bigger and bigger by the second.

Robbie took off his shirt and put it in the sink where he ran it under soapy water. But after he was done scrubbing his shirt the stain was still growing and it was bigger than EVER.

By now Robbie was starting to freak out. Robbie's mom came upstairs to give him a warm glass of milk before bedtime. But Robbie kept himself locked in his bedroom until she was gone.

As soon as the coast was clear Robbie ran to the laundry room to put his shirt in the washing machine. And he turned the dial to the strongest setting to make sure he got rid of that stain.

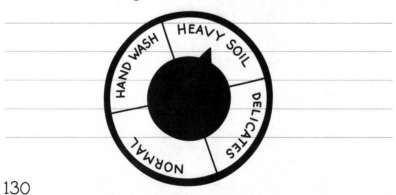

Just then Robbie's dad came into the room with a load of laundry. And Robbie was so startled that he almost jumped out of his skin.

Robbie's dad asked him what he was doing, and Robbie said he was washing some of his clothes. So Robbie's dad said he was proud of his son for becoming such a responsible young man.

That night Robbie had horrible dreams, and most of them involved strawberries.

When he woke up, his sheets were soaked with sweat. Robbie got out of bed and went to the laundry room to see if the stain was still on his shirt.

But Robbie got a terrible surprise.

His dad had put his nice dress shirts in the washing machine with Robbie's shirt, and now all the clothes were stained PINK.

Robbie decided the only thing he could do was run away. But luckily his mom caught him before he got too far.

It was time for Robbie to tell his parents the TRUTH. He confessed that the ice cream he dropped at the mall was HIS and not his dad's. Then he said he was sorry for lying about it.

Well Robbie's parents loved their son very much and they told him they were proud of him for telling the truth. They said that everyone makes mistakes but the important thing is that you LEARN from them.

And just to show how great Robbie's parents were, they took him back to the mall so they could all get ice cream together. Robbie bought three ice cream cones, all rocky road.

And this time he was extra careful not to drop any.

But Robbie forgot his dad was allergic to almonds and his father's lips swelled up like balloons. Robbie's dad had to go to the emergency room to get a shot, which made it hard for Robbie to enjoy his ice cream.

LICK

When Robbie got home he noticed a small chocolate stain on his crisp white shirt, and the whole thing started up again.

a mummy

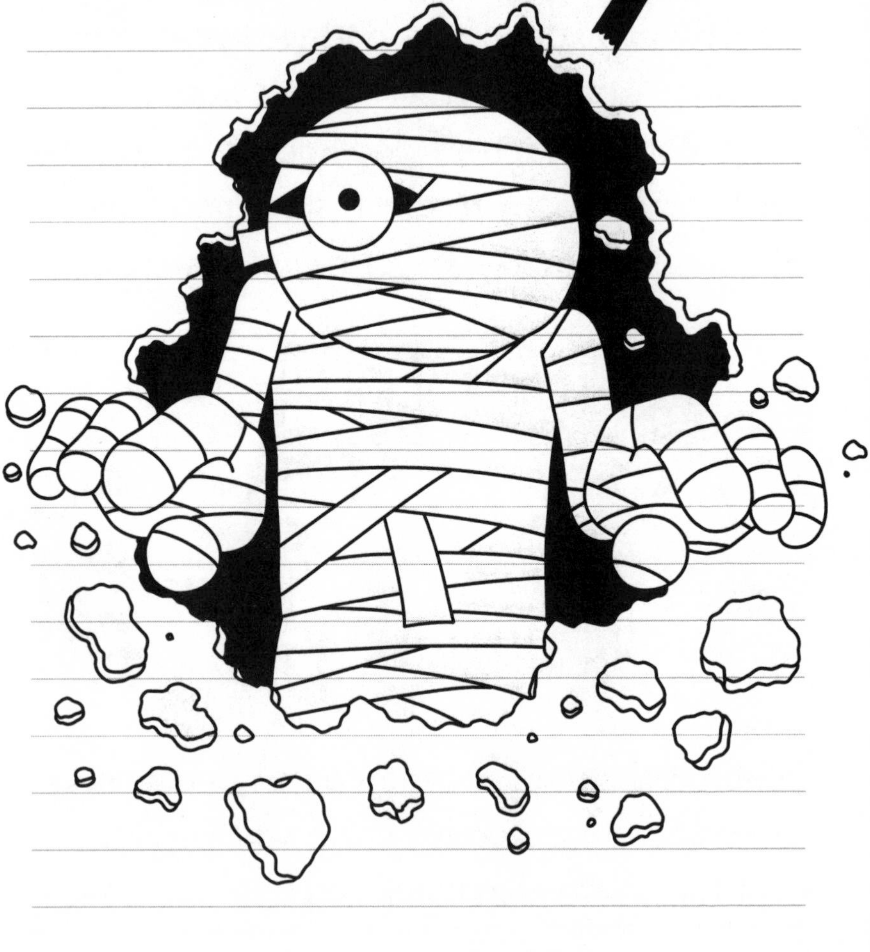

A long time ago in Ancient Egypt there lived a pharaoh named Mekh. And when Mekh died the royal priests and priestesses wrapped his body to prepare it for the afterlife.

But a few thousand years later some archaeologists from another country discovered Mekh's pyramid and took his sarcophagus with them.

When Mekh woke up he was disappointed to find out that he was in a museum and not in the afterlife like he'd expected. On top of that they didn't even put his sarcophagus in a nice spot.

So Mekh was ANGRY. And he used his mummy powers to make a big mess of things in the museum.

But even after Mekh destroyed the museum he wasn't satisfied. So he went outside and that's where he REALLY did some damage.

That night Mekh was all over the news for wrecking the city.

MUMMY'S REVENGE!

139

Mekh was just getting started though. He went from country to country destroying everything in his path, and wherever he went he made headlines.

MOMIE DÉTRUIT LA VILLE

ミイラ、東京を破壊

140

But after a while Mekh ran out of things to destroy and people started losing interest anyway.

Eventually Mekh settled down a little and tried to get used to living in the modern world. And even though he would've rather been in the afterlife he had to admit that television was a pretty great invention.

One night Mekh was watching the news and there was a story about how some archaeologists made a new discovery in Egypt. They found the tomb of Khaba, a pharaoh who lived a few thousand years ago.

NEW EGYPTIAN TOMB UNEARTHED

Well at first Mekh started getting angry because this brought back memories of what happened to HIM. But after a few minutes of deep breathing he was able to calm down.

People were excited about this new discovery because Khaba's tomb was really glitzy and full of treasures.

But everyone was nervous when they opened Khaba's sarcophagus because no one wanted a repeat of the Mekh situation.

Things were different this time around though. First of all Khaba was MUCH better preserved than Mekh. And Mekh was kind of annoyed when the people on the news kept pointing that out.

MEKH   KHABA

When Khaba stepped out of his tomb he didn't just start randomly destroying things. In fact he seemed curious about the modern world and everything in it.

Khaba started appearing on morning talk shows and before long he was everyone's favorite mummy. And Mekh never would've admitted he was jealous but he was.

In fact Khaba was so popular that people started making all sorts of mummy merchandise and used his image without asking permission.

So Khaba hired a slick lawyer and before long all that stuff was shut down. But then Khaba's lawyer took it a step further.

His lawyer trademarked "The Mummy" which made it so that Khaba was the only one who could use the name. And then she made a big announcement about it in front of the TV cameras.

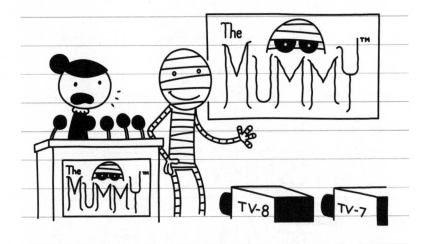

Well this really ticked off Mekh, who didn't think it was right that Khaba could do that. Plus Mekh was annoyed that he didn't think of it FIRST.

After a while Khaba had his own fashion line and kids' cereal and even a major motion picture in the works. And everywhere Mekh went there was Khaba's face.

Mekh thought it was time for HIM to cash in on this mummy craze too. So he started calling himself "The Original Mummy" and he put a few ads out there.

THE ⟨ORIGINAL⟩ MUMMY

AVAILABLE FOR:

• BIRTHDAY PARTIES

• CORPORATE EVENTS

• BAR/BAT MITZVAHS

ASK FOR MEKH

But a few weeks later Mekh got a letter from Khaba's lawyer threatening to sue him for everything he owned unless he took down the ads.

FROM LEGAL COUNSEL OF The MUMMY™

But this just made Mekh MAD. Maybe not as mad as when he used to go around destroying cities with his mummy powers but still pretty mad.

So Mekh hired a lawyer of his OWN and sued Khaba to try and stop him from calling himself The Mummy since Mekh was famous first. And it was a huge trial and everyone watched it on TV.

MUMMIES SQUARE OFF IN COURT

Well Mekh didn't have a lot of money so his lawyer wasn't as slick as Khaba's. And when the trial ended the judge ruled that Khaba was the winner.

Mekh had to agree that he'd never use the name The Original Mummy or The Classic Mummy or anything like that. In fact all he was allowed to do was call himself "a mummy" in lowercase letters.

For a while Mekh tried to make some money by calling himself "a mummy" but you really can't make any money with a name like that.

Take a picture with a mummy

$3

Mekh started working at an amusement park for Fright Nights in October. But it wasn't that much fun because it was a lot harder to scare people these days.

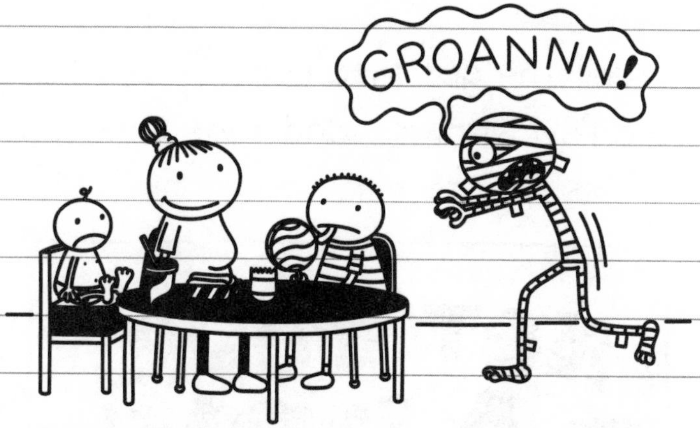
GROANNN!

Mekh still wasn't giving up though. He started calling himself The Dead Pharaoh to get around the court agreement but it turns out there was already a professional wrestler with that name and Mekh just ended up back in court.

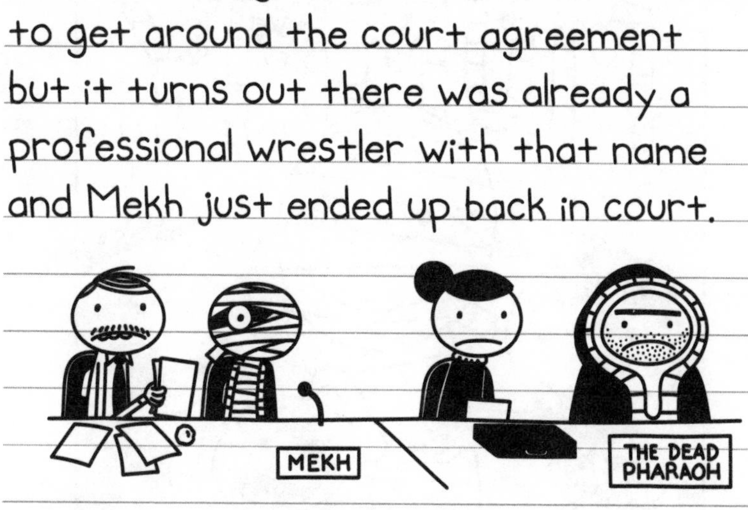
MEKH
THE DEAD PHARAOH

Things were great for Khaba for a few years but after a while the whole mummy act got stale and people stopped going to his movies.

Eventually he got into comedy but he made a few stinkers and that was the end of his film career.

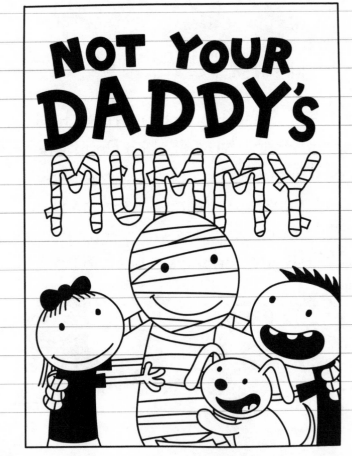

NOT YOUR DADDY's MUMMY

Then someone claimed they found a big toe in a box of Mummy Flakes and Khaba got sued for a million dollars.

And even though it turned out the person who sued him made the whole thing up, nobody would buy any food products with the word "mummy" on them after that.

Soon Khaba's money started to dry up and he couldn't afford the fancy lifestyle he was used to. After a while he had to sell his private jet and his three mansions at a discount.

Things got even worse when his wife left him and took half his money.

Khaba finally hit rock bottom when he had to sell his own sarcophagus.

But things started to turn around for Khaba when he ran into his old archenemy Mekh, who was working as a food bagger at the grocery store.

The two mummies got to talking and it turned out they had a lot more in common than they thought. Khaba and Mekh became friends and after a while Khaba moved into Mekh's apartment.

And even though they didn't always get along as roommates, the one thing they agreed on was that television really was a pretty great invention.

THE SCIENCE PROJECT

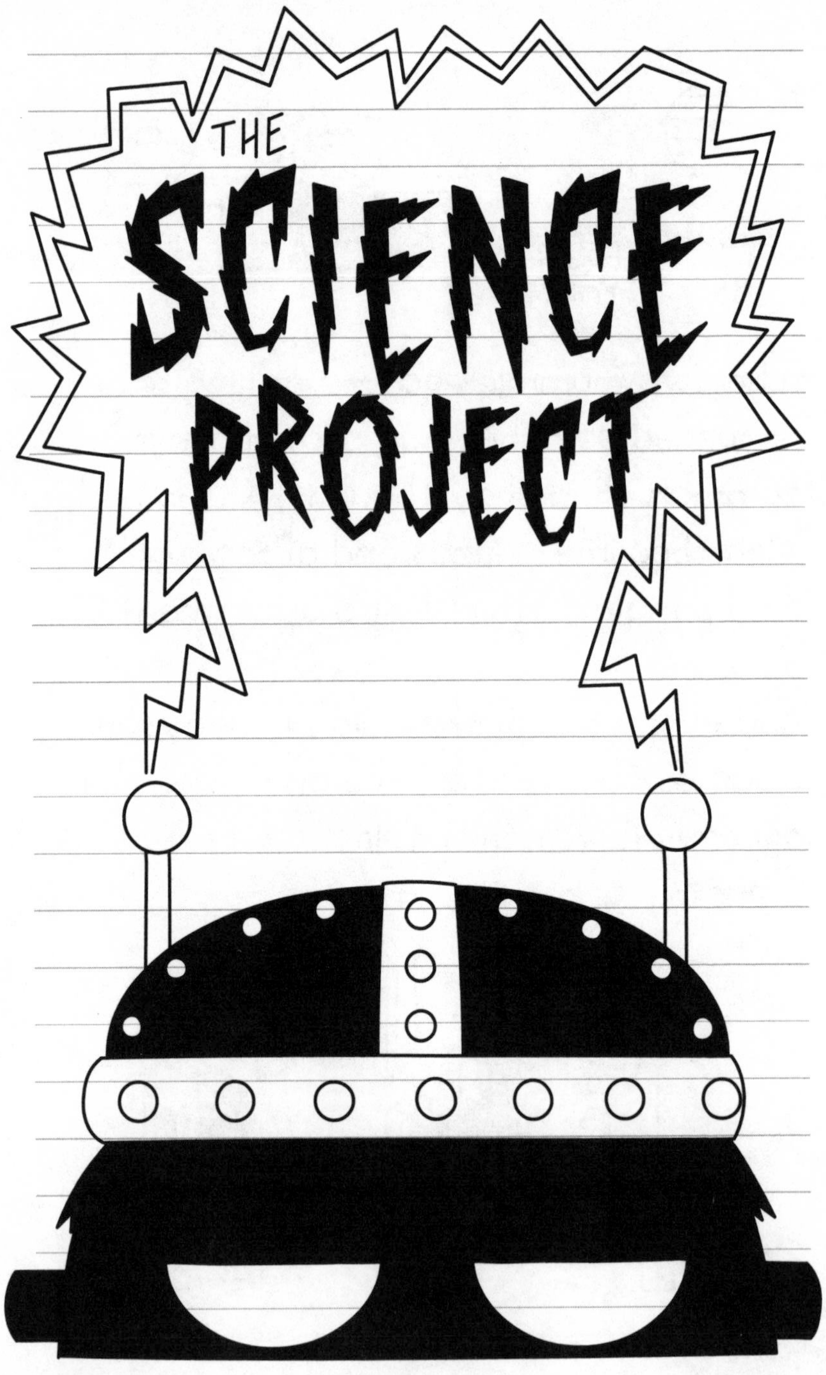

There was once a boy named Victor, and Victor was not a happy child.

This was a long time ago, before video games and TV and all that. So the only thing that Victor had to entertain himself with were books. And since his parents were both doctors, the only kinds of books they kept in the house were ones about science and medicine and stuff like that.

The other thing that made Victor sad was that his parents wouldn't let him have a pet. They told Victor he wasn't responsible enough to take care of an animal and that they'd end up doing all the work.

And even when Victor promised he'd feed his pet and take it outside three times a day the answer was always "no."

The only thing that really made Victor happy was school. He was a smart kid from reading his parents' books, and his science teacher said if he studied hard he'd be famous for his work one day.

So when it was time for the middle school Science Fair, Victor was really excited.

He worked for a whole month on his
project and he hoped it was good enough
to win first place.

But Lizzie Leggot won with a volcano
project that Victor was sure her
parents had helped her with.

So Lizzie walked away with a first place
ribbon and all Victor got was a lousy
honorable mention certificate.

From that moment on all Victor could
think about was NEXT year's Science
Fair. He read his parents' books from
front to back, trying to come up
with an idea for a new project, but he
couldn't think of anything that would
really knock people's socks off.

One day when Victor was looking out
his back window at the cemetery behind
his house he got an idea. To be honest it
was kind of a TWISTED idea, but Victor
knew if he could pull it off, his project
would win first place in the Science Fair
for SURE.

Victor did experiments in his attic every night to get ready for the Science Fair. His parents thought he was spending too much time by himself and wondered if maybe they should've let him have a pet after all.

One year later it was finally time for the big Science Fair, and Victor brought his project with him to school.

And if you want to know where Victor got the materials for his science project, let's just say sometimes it's better not to ask too many questions.

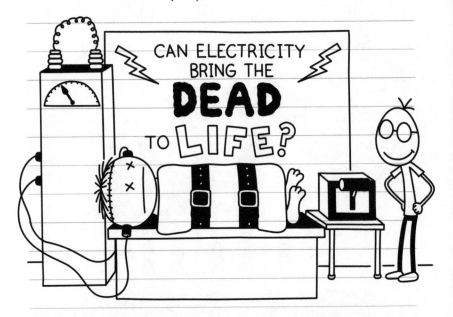

Even though Victor had been working on his project for a whole year he didn't know if it was gonna actually WORK. But he knew if it didn't he'd lose to Lizzie Leggot for the second year in a row. So when the judges gathered around his project, Victor crossed his fingers and threw the switch.

All of Victor's hard work paid off when his creation came to life. And this time Victor got the first place ribbon and Lizzie was the one who had to settle for honorable mention.

On the walk home, Victor was feeling pretty good about himself. But he kind of wished he'd thought about what was gonna happen after the Science Fair was OVER because now he didn't know what he was supposed to do with his project.

CLOMP CLOMP

Victor thought maybe he could ditch his creation at the cemetery but his science project wouldn't take the hint.

Victor picked a stick off the ground and chucked it over the cemetery gate. But his creation thought it was a GAME and brought the stick right back.

Then Victor started having FUN with his science project, and the two of them played for hours outside. And Victor found out the thing his creation liked the most was to have his belly rubbed.

Victor told his parents about his first place ribbon at the Science Fair and they were very proud of their son. And even though they were a little concerned about where Victor got the materials for his project, they knew that sometimes it's better not to ask too many questions.

Victor asked if he could keep his science project as a pet, and after he promised to feed it and take it out three times a day they finally gave in and said "yes."

From that day on Victor and his new pet were the best of friends and they never spent a day apart.

Victor became famous just like his science teacher predicted, and he was always in the paper for one thing or another.

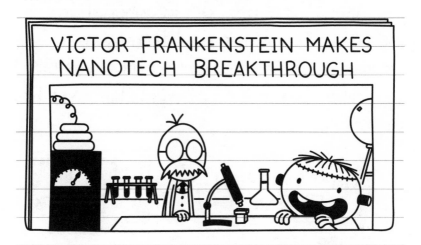

Each year Victor got a little older but his pet didn't age. And when Victor finally died his loyal sidekick was right there by his side.

Over the years people forgot all about Victor Frankenstein, but his pet became kind of famous. People called him "Frankenstein's pet" or "Frankenstein's monster," but after a while they just called him "Frankenstein." And he was OK with that but it kind of made him miss his old friend.

Frankenstein didn't know what to do with all his free time now that Victor was gone but he knew you couldn't really do anything without an education. So he went to school, starting with the first grade.

And even though he was bigger than the other kids they treated him like he was one of them.

Frankenstein was a quick learner and he actually skipped a few grades. In middle school he entered the Science Fair and took first place just like his friend Victor. And if you're wondering where he got the materials for his project, let's just say that sometimes it's better not to ask too many questions.

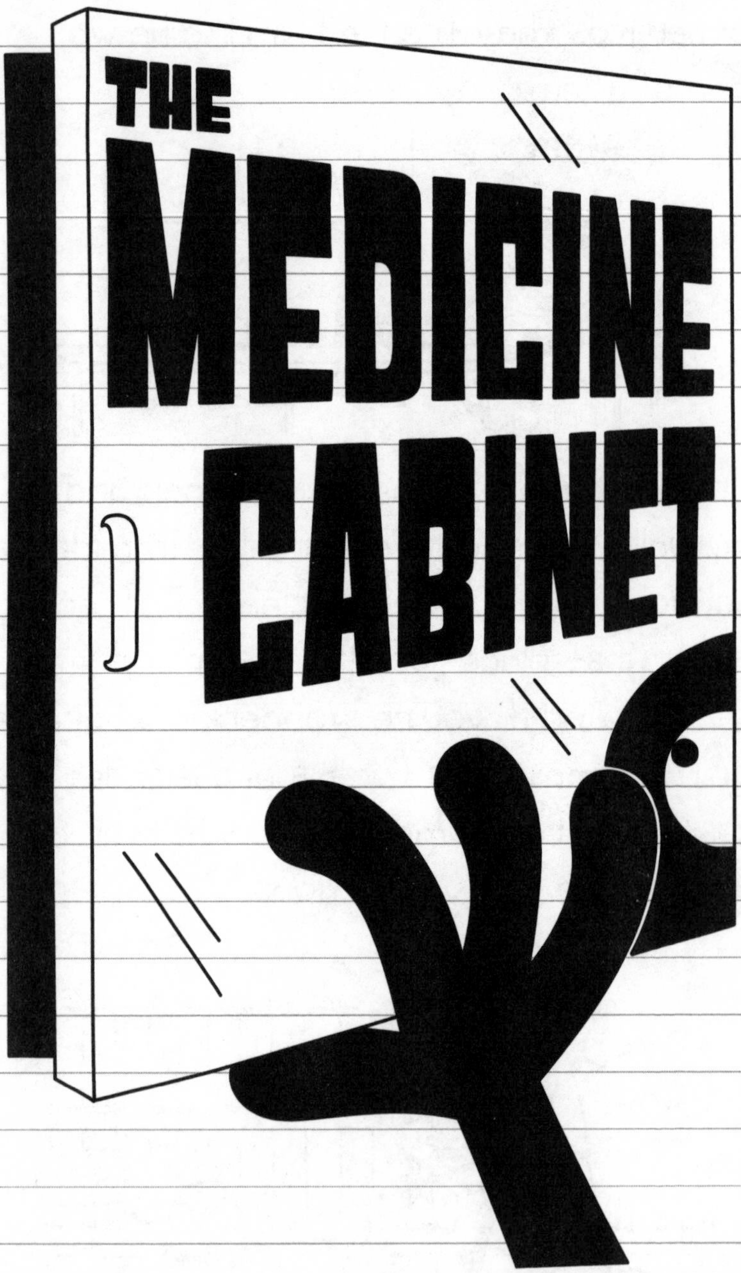
THE
MEDICINE
CABINET

Ryan was a curious boy, and he loved to explore every nook and cranny of his apartment. And even though sometimes he got into places he didn't belong, his parents never seemed to mind.

Ryan's favorite room to explore was his parents' bathroom, because they had so many interesting things in the drawers next to the sink.

Sometimes Ryan would use his mother's hairspray to make his hair stick straight up. And sometimes he'd make a foamy beard out of his father's shaving cream.

Every once in a while Ryan would put on lotion to make his skin feel extra silky. And once he covered himself in Band-Aids just because.

Ryan's parents were glad their son was a curious child and they never got mad at him for experimenting with stuff in their bathroom. But they told him he must NEVER go in their medicine cabinet.

And if you're saying "Hey this sounds just like The Cellar" well you're wrong because this story is totally different.

Anyway if there's one thing you should never tell a curious child it's where NOT to go. Because that night Ryan waited for his parents to fall asleep and then he snuck into their bathroom.

Ryan opened the door to the medicine cabinet. He was expecting to find something really interesting in there but the only things on the shelves were a pair of tweezers, nail clippers, cotton balls, and a bottle of makeup.

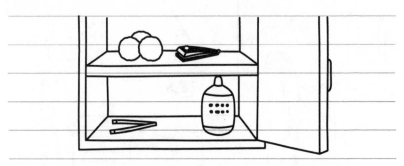

Ryan was disappointed but he decided to use the nail clippers to trim his fingernails since it had been a while. Then he dabbed some of the makeup on his cheeks just for fun.

He realized he had used up all the makeup
and now the bottle was empty. But he
didn't want to throw it in the trash
because then his parents would know he'd
disobeyed them.

So he put the bottle back in the medicine
cabinet and closed the door. Then he snuck
past his parents' bed and went to sleep
in his room.

SNEAK
SNEAK

When Ryan woke up he could smell the
bacon and eggs his mom was cooking in
the kitchen. He went into his parents'
bathroom to brush his teeth just like
he always did. But when he looked in the
mirror something seemed DIFFERENT.

Ryan's hair looked a few shades lighter,
like it did when he was a little kid.
And his freckles were back too. But
the weirdest thing was that his head
seemed smaller than usual.

Now Ryan was getting kind of nervous.
He opened the medicine cabinet and took
a closer look at that bottle of makeup.
And when he read the label he started to
REALLY freak out.

Just then Ryan's mom called him from the kitchen and said breakfast was ready. Ryan didn't want his parents to see him looking like he did because then they'd know he'd gone in the medicine cabinet. So he put on a hoodie and kept it on while he ate his breakfast.

Ryan's mom always gave him a kiss before he went to school. But today Ryan rushed out the door before she had a chance.

On the way to school Ryan felt a little dizzy. He checked his reflection in a window but then he wished he DIDN'T. Because now he looked even younger than he did before.

So Ryan put his hood back on and planned to wear it for the rest of the day.

But Ryan's teacher Miss Pickler didn't
allow kids to keep their hoods on in class
and she asked him to please remove it.

Ryan was hoping the other kids wouldn't
notice he looked a little different. But
kids always pick up on those kinds of
things.

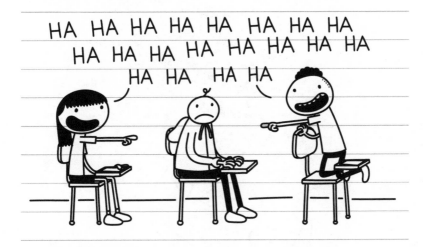

Miss Pickler didn't even seem surprised though. She asked Ryan to come to the front of the room. Then she handed him a small package and told him he should take it to the restroom.

When Ryan opened the package there was a bar of soap along with a note.

MAKEUP REMOVER FORMULA

Get soap wet in the sink.

Rub hands on soap to make a sudsy lather.

Scrub face with soap suds.

Rinse face clean.

Good luck! ♡ Miss P.

SOAP

Ryan was glad Miss Pickler had experience with this kind of thing. He followed the instructions and had to repeat the steps a few times to get all the makeup off.

But even though Miss Pickler's secret formula stopped him from getting any younger it didn't get him back to looking like his old self.

On the walk home Ryan realized he was gonna have to tell his parents the truth about what he did. But when he got to his apartment there were two old people in the kitchen who he didn't recognize.

This day had already been hard enough for Ryan so he just sort of lost it.

But it turns out the old people were his PARENTS. They asked Ryan to sit down so they could explain what was happening.

Ryan's mom and dad said they had him later in life and had been using that magic age-reversing makeup because they didn't want to look older than all the OTHER parents.

Ryan asked his parents how old they were and they said 114 and 112. And Ryan thought that really was pretty old but he didn't want to hurt their feelings.

Ryan's parents said since he used up all the makeup they were stuck looking like this for good. But Ryan said he didn't care HOW old they looked because he loved them no matter what.

And from then on things were pretty great for Ryan and his family. Sometimes people looked at them a little funny but they didn't really care because they had each other and that was all that mattered.

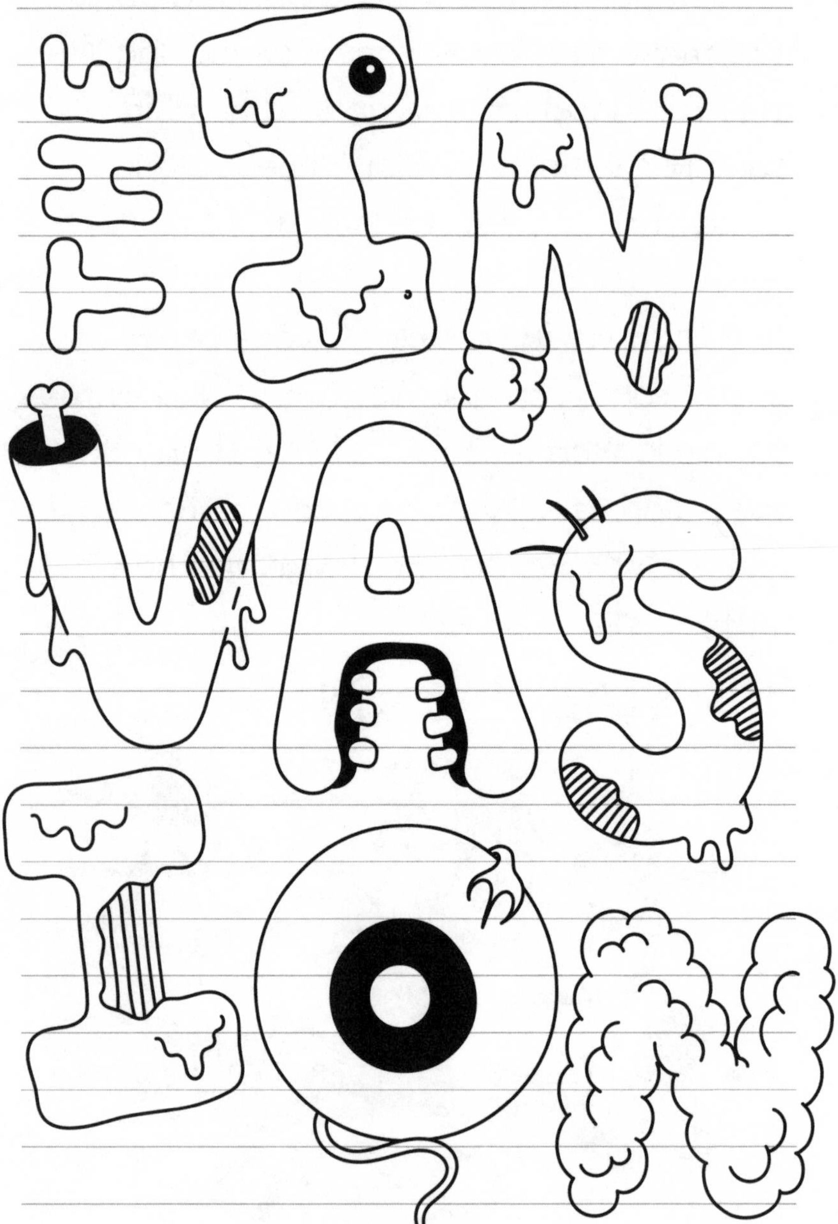
THE INVASION

The people of Fairview were some of the happiest people on Earth. They lived in a beautiful, clean city and everyone was nice to their neighbors.

One day news came that there was a zombie invasion in a city on the other side of the world.

But the city was very far away and
the people of Fairview just went back
to their normal lives. And even when the
zombie invasion spread, people didn't
pay that much attention because it
didn't seem like something so awful could
happen in a place as nice as Fairview.

But when the city next door to Fairview
got invaded by zombies there was no
ignoring the problem anymore.

The mayor had a big meeting and
everybody discussed what they should do.

The military wanted to blast the zombies with their weapons. But then someone said that wouldn't work since zombies were already dead.

The scientists wanted to build a giant force field around the city to keep the zombies out. And even though it was a cool idea everyone agreed it would take too long to figure out how to do it.

Someone said that the only thing zombies wanted was brains so maybe they should just feed the scientists to the zombies. And everyone liked that idea except the scientists.

After the mayor listened to everyone's ideas he told them his own idea.

He said that every city that had tried to keep the zombies out had failed, and there was nothing they could do to stop the zombies from invading the city.

So his idea was to let them IN.

At first everyone thought that was the dumbest idea they ever heard. But then the mayor told them part two of his plan.

He said since zombies were so crazy about brains, they could use plastic molds to make FAKE brains out of something like tofu.

People still thought it was a pretty dumb idea but they couldn't see any other options. And a few days later when the zombies finally arrived the people of Fairview were ready for them.

At first the zombies were confused because they were used to people putting up more of a fight.

But it didn't really make a difference
to the zombies because they were only
there for one thing.

Just then the mayor gave the green
light and the food trucks rolled in.

Well it turned out that the zombies liked the tofu brains as much as the real thing. So zombies just like food that's SHAPED like brains, the way little kids like food shaped like dinosaurs.

CHEW CHEW

CHOMP SMACK

GOBBLE SLURP

And if someone had figured that out years earlier there would've been a lot fewer problems between people and zombies.

The zombies liked the tofu brains so much that they decided to stick around Fairview. And nobody seemed to mind because they were just glad the zombies weren't eating THEM.

After a while things started to go back to normal in the city of Fairview. And life was pretty much the way it was before, only now with zombies.

In fact things were pretty great. A lot of the zombies got jobs and they used the money they earned to buy houses.

People and zombies realized they had a lot in common and their families started having playdates together.

Zombie kids went to school where they learned to talk like humans. And humans learned to talk like zombies, which wasn't really all that hard.

🍎	apple	brainnns
🍌	banana	braains
🐱	cat	brrainss

Humans discovered that they liked brain-shaped food just as much as the zombies did. And before long, drive-through places were cropping up everywhere.

Zombies started getting elected to important positions, and soon the city of Fairview had its first zombie mayor.

So everything was pretty great in Fairview. But one day the skies darkened and a giant spaceship appeared above the city.

At first everyone was freaking out about the spaceship because no one knew why it was there. Then the new mayor held a meeting to figure out what to do.

The military said they should use all their weapons and blast the spaceship out of the sky. And a lot of people liked that idea.

But the scientists said the aliens probably had superior weapons so attacking them wasn't a good idea. They said they should build a giant force field around the city to keep the aliens OUT.

And then everyone started arguing and the meeting got a little ugly.

The mayor had to step in to calm everyone down. Then she gave a speech.

She reminded everyone about how the people of Fairview wanted to keep the zombies out of the city, and how great everything was now that people and zombies were living together in peace.

She said the city of Fairview was big enough for EVERYONE and that the smart thing to do was to let the aliens IN.

People got really choked up over the mayor's speech and they got behind her plan. And the next day the city rolled out the red carpet for the aliens.

Well there are two kinds of aliens, the good kind and the bad kind. And unfortunately for the citizens of Fairview these aliens were the BAD kind.

The aliens were used to people putting up more of a fight but they were fine with doing this the easy way for once.

After a while things started to go back to normal in the city of Fairview. And life was pretty much the way it was before, only now with aliens.

And even though the aliens wiped out all the humans and the zombies, they kept the drive-through restaurants. Because they were crazy for those tofu brains.

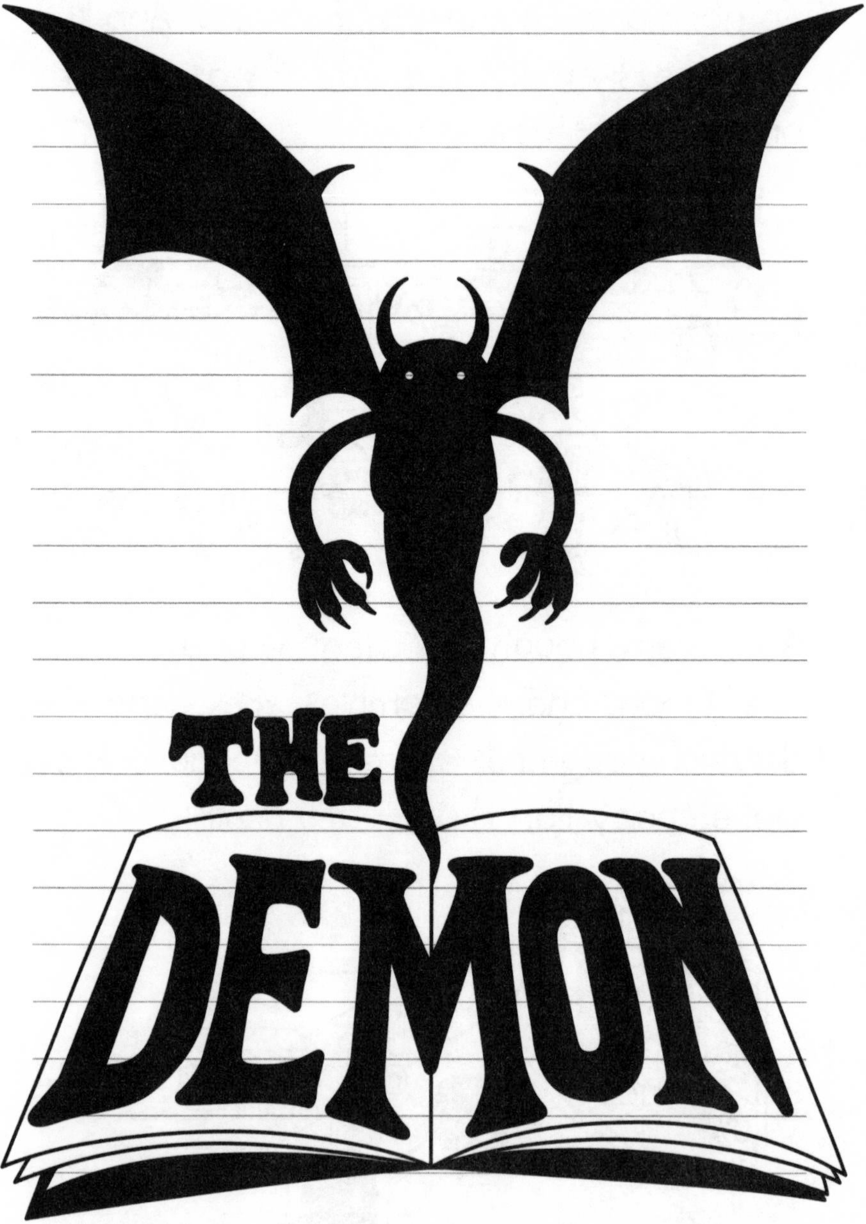
THE
DEMON

OK so maybe a few of the stories in this book are just make-believe but I promise this next one is 100 percent TRUE. And I know because it happened to ME.

Well technically it happened to me AND my best friend Greg Heffley. But there are probably some parts he can't remember so you'll have to trust me that I'm telling you the TRUTH.

This happened over the summer when Greg came to my house for a sleepover. And it was a pretty big deal because it was our first one since we got in trouble for sneaking out the last time.

My dad made us both promise we would be in bed by 10:00 p.m. And that was fine with me since I start getting sleepy at 9:30 anyway.

At 7:00 my mom came down to the basement with a big tub of arts and crafts supplies so we'd have something to do. And I was excited because I could see there were two new bottles of glitter glue in the tub.

But when my mom left, Greg said arts and crafts were for babies and we needed to do something that was actually FUN. Which kind of stunk because I didn't even get to use the glitter glue.

Then Greg pulled something out of his bag. It looked like a scary movie and Greg said he took it from his brother Rodrick's room.

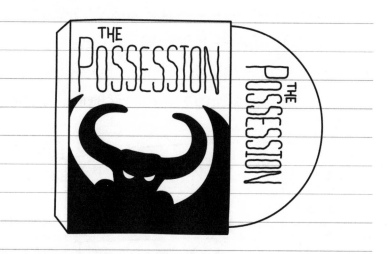

I said it looked a little TOO scary for me and maybe we should watch the one that my mom and dad just got me.

But Greg said this was a sleepover not school and he put his movie in the player.

Well I really wished we had stuck with the arts and crafts because Greg's movie was totally TERRIFYING. It was about these teenagers who find a book with ancient writing and scary pictures inside.

And when one of the teenagers reads the writing out loud the book releases a DEMON.

Then the demon gets INSIDE one of the teenagers and gives him evil powers.

And don't even ask me how the movie
ended because I made Greg shut it off
halfway through.

I thought Greg was gonna say I was
a chicken for bailing out but he said
the movie was terrible and the special
effects looked totally FAKE. Plus he
said the story didn't make any sense
because the teenager who got possessed
wouldn't have known how to read the
words in an ancient book.

Well the special effects looked pretty
real to ME, but I guess Greg had a point
about the ancient language thing.

I asked him if a person could get
possessed by a demon in real life and
Greg said that was fake too.

Then he said he'd PROVE it to me and he started saying the words those teenagers read out loud.

At first nothing happened and I thought Greg was probably right about the movie being fake. But then Greg's body started to twitch and when he opened his eyes he seemed TOTALLY different.

So now my best friend was possessed by a DEMON. And I knew if my parents found out they'd never let us have another sleepover again.

I was hoping the demon would snap out of it and go back to being Greg but he didn't. And he made a mess of the shelves that me and my mom had spent the whole afternoon organizing.

Then the demon noticed the arts-and-crafts bin and before I could stop him he went totally CRAZY with the glitter glue.

After the demon was done wrecking the basement he headed upstairs. And he must've had supernatural strength or something because I couldn't slow him down.

And if you thought the demon made a mess of the basement then you should've seen what he did to the KITCHEN.

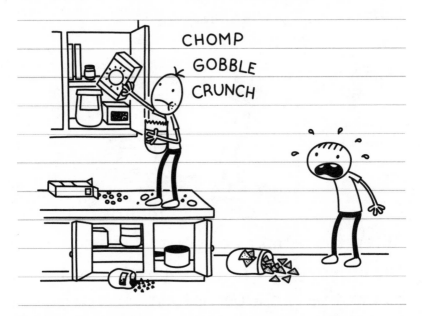

CHOMP
GOBBLE
CRUNCH

I was nervous my parents were gonna wake up because the demon was making a huge racket and their bedroom was right above the kitchen. So I needed to figure out how to fix this situation QUICK.

Now I really wished we'd watched that movie all the way to the end to see how those teenagers got rid of the demon.

But I couldn't go back downstairs to finish the movie because I didn't want to leave the demon by himself. Luckily Mom's laptop was on the kitchen counter so I did a quick search. But I couldn't find any straight answers and it seemed like you might need a professional anyway.

SEARCH: how to get rid of a demon

SEARCH RESULTS (2,432,217 matches)

Laying on of hands
Ritual performed by priest
Using holy water
Herbal use in dispelling bad energy

AD Find an exorcist in your area!

One of the websites said you could get rid of a demon with holy water but it was almost 10:00 at night and I was pretty sure the church was closed at that hour.

After the demon finished emptying
out the kitchen cabinets he started to
come after ME. And it's hard to stay
quiet when you're being chased around
a kitchen island by an evil spirit who's
chucking eggs at you.

Luckily the demon slipped on some baking
soda on the floor and that gave me a
chance to ESCAPE. So I ran into the
bathroom and locked the door.

I didn't want the demon to know I was in there so I turned off the lights and stayed as quiet as I could. But demons must have supernatural smelling or something because it didn't take him long to figure out where I was.

I was afraid he was gonna use his fire breath to burn down the door. But it got quiet for a while and that made me EXTRA nervous.

Then I heard a weird rattling noise coming from the doorknob.

Somehow the demon had figured out how to pick the LOCK with a paper clip.

The next thing I knew the demon was turning the doorknob. The only thing I had to defend myself with was a toilet brush, so I dipped it in the toilet bowl and sprayed the demon with water.

It turns out you don't need to use actual holy water to get rid of a demon. Because a few seconds later Greg was back to his regular self.

The bad news is that all the noise woke up my parents and they sent Greg home. But that was OK with me because the truth is I start to get sleepy at 9:30 anyway.

WELL I WARNED YOU

OK so maybe I shouldn't have written those scary stories because now I'M a little spooked. And it probably wasn't such a smart idea to write down that demon spell in here because that could cause all sorts of problems.

But I'm gonna show this book to Greg anyway because I have a feeling he'll really like it.